A COLD CHILL CLUNG TO HER SKIN LIKE AN ICY RASH. She trembled violently beneath it. *Call help*, she thought. *Figure this out later, but for now, call help. You're alone in the house.*

Mandy approached the desk as she might a hive of bees. Slow steps brought her shaking to the edge. She snatched the cell phone from the desk, then leaped back. She fumbled the device open and punched in 911, then hit send and put the phone to her ear.

"Still want to chat on the phone?" a high rasping voice asked. Then a piercing stutter erupted through the speaker.

"Hahahahahahahahahahaha . . ."

BY
STEFAN PETRUCHA
AND THOMAS PENDLETON

HARPER TEEN
AN IMPRINT OF HARPERCOLLINSPUBLISHERS

Grateful acknowledgment is given to Shaun O'Boyle
for the use of the title page image, © Shaun O'Boyle.
More of his evocative images can be seen at
www.oboylephoto.com.

HarperTeen is an imprint of
HarperCollins Publishers.

Library of Congress Cataloging-in-Publication Data
Petrucha, Stefan.
Lurker / by Stefan Petrucha and Thomas Pendleton. —
1st ed.
p.   cm. — (Wicked dead ; 1)
Summary: Four ghost girls, trapped in an abandoned
orphanage, relate the story of high school student Mandy,
who becomes caught up in a terrifying encounter after
one of her classmates is tragically murdered.
ISBN 978-0-06-113849-2 (pbk.)
[1. Supernatural—Fiction. 2. Murder—Fiction. 3. Horror
stories.] I. Pendleton, Thomas, 1965- II. Title.
PZ7.P44727Lu 2007   2007014470
[Fic]—dc22   CIP
                                              AC

Typography by Christopher Stengel
❖
First Edition

THOMAS PENDLETON dedicates this book to JCP and all the *wicked* ones the world over.

STEFAN PETRUCHA dedicates this book to the dead—Martin, Felicia, Amelia, Michael, Frank, Mary, Joseph L., and the many others he does not know. He hopes you've all got a great game going somewhere.

PROLOGUE

At the end of a long field of dead grass otherwise surrounded by forest, the six-story Georgian mansion jutted up on the horizon. Huge and vacant, glass gone from most windows, it seemed held up by the pregnant clouds that swirled in the darkening sky. Its rotted front doors, tall and wide enough for an SUV to pass through, were bracketed by flattened columns. Atop these sat a triangular cornice, the letters on its lowest beam still reading Lockwood Orphanage—a name that had seemingly outlived its purpose, for now the house appeared as abandoned as its former occupants.

When evening approached and the rain began, when the winds yowled and the thunder boomed, the dark inside the gutted rooms became a great and wonderful thing. Deeper than the storm, deeper than the growing night, it covered everything completely: moldering furniture, rotted toys and schoolbooks, the history, the decay, even the bits of nature that had creeped in over the years.

But no dark is perfect. A small circle of yellow light stuck out on the enormous stairs in the main hall like a speck on a blank sheet of paper. It moved down, a single step at a single time, slowly at first, then faster and faster, as if once confident it was alone, it felt a need for speed.

"As long as you insist on holding the lamp, Mary, could you at least slow down for the rest of us?" Daphne whispered as she caught up with the light. Her voice was soft, straining to be gentle, but it was still more a command than a request. She was a tall girl, severe, with sharp, short brown hair and a pointed nose. She wore what looked like striped men's pajamas. On someone else, they might have looked clownish, but somehow they only added to her air of authority.

Mary turned and answered, "All right." As she did, the gold ringlets of the petite girl's hair picked up the light from the old oil lamp she held, giving her pale white face a curved, irregular frame.

But Mary didn't slow enough, so Daphne put a hand out to stop her completely. Now the lamp swung slightly, illuminating Mary's long, flowing nightdress, parts of which were nearly transparent, revealing a bit of shoulder and some slight cleavage. With Mary motionless, two more girls emerged from the black, and all four figures huddled quietly together on the stairs, their whispers muffled by the storm.

"Do you have to always bring that stupid lantern? The oil smells like fish. Can't we at least find a flashlight? It isn't the Middle Ages anymore, you know."

This from Anne, who seemed to be the same age as Mary but couldn't have been more different. Even the long black T-shirt she wore for pajamas seemed defiant and annoyed in the way it refused to just slip into shadow.

"It's hardly stupid," Mary objected. "I like the soft light it casts, and besides, it's a tradition. If you don't like it, hold your nose."

The objection at least temporarily squelched, the foursome proceeded down the stairs, footsteps as quiet as their breath. It wasn't until they hit the final step that a distant wooden creak made them pause again, this time all at once.

"What was that?" said Shirley, poking her head up above her slumped shoulders. The mousy redhead's eyes darted this way and that, searching the gloom.

"Just the rats," Daphne answered. She said this quickly, as if to beat out Anne, who looked about to say something hurtful.

With that, the four reached the floor. Staying close to one another, they drifted across a cavernous space, maneuvering around tattered furniture and wide dangerous gaps in the wooden floor. By and by they reached the rough center of the great room.

Mary set the lamp on the dust-frosted planks, then walked toward one of the few windows that wasn't broken or boarded up. Leaning into the tall old glass, resting her forehead on its coolness, she peered up through black trees to the anxious gray clouds.

"What are you doing?" Shirley asked, shaking the sleeve of her long, high-necked wool nightgown for better biting access to a pinky nail. "Should you be doing that? Shouldn't we get started?"

"Shh. It's all right," Mary said. "The storm is loud

and we're safe. Listen. You can hear the thicker drops crashing through the leaves, thudding into the dirt like insect meteorites."

Anne rolled her eyes. "Wow. Freak much? Can't you just call rain, rain?"

Mary flashed her a glance. "No," she answered. "Because then it would just be rain."

She turned back to the window and continued listening, out of spite, it seemed.

"I love the thunder," Mary said wistfully. "I love to watch the lightning play among the clouds in the heavens, and dart in jagged figures upon the piny hills."

Anne plopped down on an ancient couch and crossed her arms across her chest. "Whenever you're ready, Emily Dickinson."

"What's the hurry, Anne? Are you writing a book?" Shirley said, poking her head up. Tickled by her comment, she sat on the floor and started biting the nail of her right thumb, working it back and forth as she nibbled.

"'Are you writing a book?'" Anne shot back, mocking the whiny voice. "What exactly does that mean, anyway? Or is it just one of those things you like to say?"

"Let her alone," Daphne said, breaking her recent silence and striding fully into the lamplight. It revealed a bit of the curvy figure that filled out the hips and chest of the male pajamas. Though she didn't seem older than the others, she spoke as if she were the only adult. "We don't want any screaming, do we?"

As Anne's eyes clamped shut in annoyance, Shirley stuck her tongue out, long and pink. Mary stifled a giggle.

"I don't like to rush. I like to talk a little first, that's all," Shirley said, lowering her eyes. "It helps soothe me."

"Can't have Miss Delicate tense," Anne said, glaring at Shirley.

Mary finally turned from the window. "You heard Daphne. That's enough. You're only in a state because it hasn't been your turn for a while. No one blames you for that. But attacking Shirley because you know she gets afraid, or me because I don't care to argue, is cowardice. Why don't you toss some of your clever barbs at Daphne?"

Anne eyed Mary coolly. She looked as if she were about to say something, but Daphne stepped between them.

"Yes, Anne. Why *don't* you?"

The bitter girl made a face, then flipped her hand in the air in a gesture of temporary surrender.

A sound echoed in the great room, another wooden tick that could have been the old boards settling, or creaking in the wind, or not.

This time Anne snapped her head around and said, "What *was* that?"

"Still just rats . . . probably," Daphne said, but even she looked up and peered through the darkness, searching it.

"It couldn't be her," Mary said. "The storm is loud tonight."

The other three felt Shirley stiffen at that. Her head rose from between her slumped shoulders as if her whole body was tensed for flight.

Daphne petted her hair and smiled. "Don't worry. We're fine. Mary's right about the storm."

Shirley gave off a little laugh. She shivered and hugged herself, then said, "Rats," and shivered again as if pleased to be scaring herself in just a small way. "Rats."

"Sit down, Mary," Daphne said. "You, too, Anne, by the lamp. We can chat a little more, but we should at least sit down together." She folded her long legs as she nestled onto the floor. "This time you sit next to me, Shirley, so I don't have to hear Anne moan if she doesn't win again."

Anne rose, her black T-shirt making her torso briefly invisible against the dark behind it, and said, "Fine, but Shirley better stop laughing through her nose. Last time she blew a chunk of snot into my lap."

Mary and Daphne smiled at that, but Shirley bristled. "I did not!"

They all took their places, sitting cross-legged on the floor. Mary and Daphne flanked Shirley to keep the girl feeling as calm and comfortable as possible.

Settling in, Mary rubbed her hand in a small circle on the floor in front of her. "Rats. I hate the vile animals."

"Because you think *we're* all about souls, that people are better. Don't underestimate the rats," Anne said with a smile. "There's a lot of power in pure hunger. A lot of pleasure, too."

Mary stiffened. "I don't underestimate animals. I simply choose, if at all possible, not to become one."

"All right, girls," Daphne announced. "Since Anne is in one of her moods, I guess we've had enough chitchat. It's time. I've got the Clutch."

"Well, at least *you* didn't lose it," Anne said, casting a look at Shirley.

Shirley seemed offended. She spat out a piece of nail and announced, "I've never lost the Clutch!"

"No, it only took you an hour to find the last time you hid it," Anne said.

"It did not!" Shirley answered loudly. "Not an hour!"

"Shh. Don't waste your energy, either of you," Daphne said, sounding somewhat motherly, but really more like a boss. "After all, it could be your turn tonight."

Shirley shrugged, bit at another nail, and mumbled, "I don't see it. I haven't had a turn in days either."

"And how happy are we for that?" Anne asked with a sneer.

That was all the abuse even the mousy girl could take. At once, Shirley reared, her woolen gown unfolding as she rose, eyes widening as if she were a crazed bird, head shaking. Mary gasped, but Daphne, somehow faster than Shirley, managed to rise behind her and gently, but firmly, push her back down.

"Annie, that wasn't very nice, or very smart. We've agreed to support each other. To wish each other the best, not tear each other down."

"Right. I forgot the warm and fuzzy Oprah crap," Anne said, and looked away. "Well, give them here. My turn to open the bag."

Shirley seemed defiant a moment, as if still in the thrall of her sudden rage, then sighed and let her shoulders slump back into their usual position. Daphne drew a vermilion bag from the pocket of her men's pajamas and held it toward Anne.

"Take it, then."

Anne reached forward and snatched the bag. The sudden move rumpled her T-shirt, so she had to adjust it as she sat back down, legs crossed, her pale knees sticking out from beneath the folds of the shirt.

Everyone stared at the Clutch as Anne's eager fingers unraveled the knot in the golden string that held it closed. As she upended it, hard, ivory shapes tumbled onto the floor between them.

They looked like bones, little ones. Animal bones, perhaps, or carved from something larger. Each had a shape: a tiny jawless skull, a thigh, a small spine, and more—five in all. There were dark lines on the faces of each, carved symbols.

Anne was staring—they were *all* staring—at the bones.

"Shirley goes first tonight," Mary said, snapping them out of what started to look like a trance.

Shirley's face remained solemn. She gingerly picked them up and pressed them between her small hands, gently rolling them back and forth across her palms. She held her hands out as if at the end of a prayer, then separated them, letting the bones just drop. They fell in a tight pack, almost clumped together, making hardly a sound on the floorboards.

The girls all leaned forward. Mary was the first to shake her head. "No."

Shirley pouted, deeply disappointed.

Daphne moved things along. "Who's next? Anne, isn't it?"

Anne rolled her eyes and grumbled.

"What's wrong now?" Mary said. "Are you going to be like this all night? You're lucky to be second."

Anne scowled as she scooped up the bones. "Oh, right. Anyone remember someone going second and winning? I don't. Second blows. First and third. That's always best."

"It seems petty to keep score," Mary said. "Besides, any time we see a pattern like that, it changes. Lightning never strikes twice. The only pattern that stays the same is the one that always wins. Three of that same mark."

Anne grunted, neither agreeing nor disagreeing. She cupped the bones and shook them vigorously. The things chittered in the hollow of her hands; then she tossed them. Unlike Shirley's gentle drop that had caused the bones to land more or less together, Anne's throw made them explode on the floor and fly in all directions. Again they all leaned forward, but this time they waited until the thigh bone slowed its spin enough to read.

"Wrong again, Anne," Shirley said, pulling free a nail-shard from her thumb. "You win. Happy now?"

"Thrilled. It's about damn time," Anne said, with a half chuckle. "Sorry for being so bitchy." She leaned forward and pinched Shirley on the cheek. "With any luck you won't have to put up with me much longer. But since that isn't likely, I can at least try to scare the pee out of you again."

Shirley swatted the hand away, then frowned and sort of folded into herself, lowering her cheek into the high collar of her woolen gown. "Why are the stories always so terrible?"

"Because life is terrible," Anne said.

"But our stories, should we ever find them, will they be terrible too?" Mary said. "Shirley's right. Murder, suicide, rape, incest—we've told the rats in these walls so many horrid things."

Anne, considerably cheerier, now mocked Mary's genteel tone as she had Shirley's whine before. "Oh, but Mary, you know as well as I that these are mere decor. One must whittle one's little finger past the muscle and the bone to get to the bloody heart of things."

"Enough," Daphne said. "The night doesn't last forever, ladies. Why don't you get started, Anne?"

Though grammatically a question, it didn't sound like a request, but an order. Anne just nodded and looked down at the bones, studying them, absorbing something from them. Her brow, for the first time, knitted, and the previously catty girl fell deep into thought.

Seeing Anne quieted seemed to delight Shirley, who grinned, though she tried to hide it. After a while, head still down, gnawed fingernail still near her mouth, she said, "Have you got it?"

"Yeah," Anne said, raising an eyebrow as she

settled back on her haunches.

The others shifted briefly, trying to find the most comfortable position.

Then Anne began the story, and it went something like this. . . .

No one at Lake Crest High was surprised when Nicolette Bennington didn't show up for classes that Wednesday morning. Nicki, or Naughty Nic as she was called in whispers behind her back, skipped classes all the time. If she wasn't in trouble at school, then she found trouble at home or in the world at large. It was all very fascinating and/or amusing to her peers because Naughty Nic was fun. She didn't pull lame pranks that hurt people's feelings, but she had a knack for shaking things up. Once, she pretended to be blind and walked her dad's Great Dane, Hamlet, through the mall and into the food court, where he promptly peed on the condiment stand. At Lady Foot Locker,

Hamlet found himself with a taste for a Reebok running shoe, which he grabbed off a plastic stand and proceeded to gnaw with much glee. When a salesclerk ran up and snatched the wet leather wad from Hamlet's lips, Naughty Nic handed him a credit card and said, "I'm sorry, but he's kind of doing you a favor. Nobody's wearing those anymore."

Cathy Lynn Baker was there, trying on a pair of sneakers she needed for tennis. She swore that's exactly what happened. Mandy was there, too. She was in the mall outside the shop with her friends, struck motionless by the sight of Naughty Nic in sunglasses acting like Ray Charles while Hamlet licked his lips and chomped his jaws, spraying spit all over the fat salesman in the referee shirt. Mandy did not, however, hear Nicki's clever response to the angry ref, though she told everyone at school she had. It just made a better story that way.

Sometimes, Naughty Nic showed up in the middle of a class, telling some wicked stupid story about why she was late, and other times she raised her hand to interrupt a teacher, announced "gyno appointment," and excused herself for the afternoon. She dismissed most boys as puppies: cute and amusing but messy and untrained. Word around Lake Crest was that she dated only college boys.

Mandy had three classes with Nicki, and one of them was first period gym on Wednesdays. That morning, Mandy showed up bleary eyed. She hadn't gotten much sleep and was without caffeine. On Mondays, Wednesdays, and Fridays she sacrificed her morning latte because, earlier that semester, she almost blew one all over the gymnasium floor while doing laps. So with no critical bean in her veins, Mandy trudged, shoe soles squeaking, across the shiny, waxed floor and took her place beside Laurel Wheeler, where she sighed and crossed her arms over her chest.

"Someone's looking tragic," Laurel whispered.

"Bite my soft parts, L."

"Ooo, and in such a good mood," her friend said with a laugh. "Did Dale keep you up late?"

"Incorrect, but thank you for playing."

Dale wasn't likely to be keeping her up late at all. Not anymore. Not after last night.

She was just being romantic. Impulsive. Mandy stopped by his house to surprise Dale, and while waiting in his room, found an open instant message window on his monitor, in which Dale—King Looz of Low Life—was asking some girl to come over and "watch movies." He had acted like it was no big thing, infuriating Mandy, who proceeded to dump his ass. She'd spent most of the night running angry conversations through her head and devising creative tortures. So, in a way, he had kept her up late. Something else he was not to be forgiven for.

Then, that morning, while Mandy was crossing the school parking lot, he had the nerve to just walk up and start talking to her like nothing happened. What an ass.

"I've deleted him from my buddy list."

Laurel's eyes lit up, and she bent close. "You're breaking up? No way! Why didn't you call me?"

Because she'd been IMing with their other friend, Drew, for three hours chatting about what a jerk Dale was, and by the time she'd signed off her mom was standing in the doorway obnoxiously tapping her watch. Besides, she had wanted to be sure she was deleting Dale totally before telling Laurel anything. Laurel was the goddess of text messaging, and pretty soon every cell phone at Lake Crest would be buzzing. In fact, Mandy could already see Laurel fidgeting, wanting to get to her

18

locker, her purse, her Nokia.

Just to make things more interesting, Mandy said, "Please don't tell anyone."

Laurel twitched like she had something in her eye; then her face grew serious and concerned. She wrapped a skinny arm over Mandy's shoulder and pulled her into a hug. "This is just between us, girl."

Yeah, right.

"So what happened?" Laurel asked.

The door of the boys' locker room creaked open, and Mr. Lombard waddled in, wearing a white polo shirt and baggy blue sweatpants. Their gym teacher was a pudgy little man who looked like Santa Claus without a beard. His shiny bald head had a fringe of white hair that hung too long in the back, and his cheeks always had a red tinge, which Laurel assured Mandy was from chugging too much gin and juice. Despite his alleged alcoholism, Lombard wasn't bad. He didn't bark at them like Crawford had during sophomore year and he kept up with fitness trends, so classes were sometimes interesting. Before Christmas break, they'd actually done yoga. More often than not, he smiled a lot and coached the girls, urging them on rather than making them feel crappy for not being able to climb a rope or throw a ball.

Today, though, Mandy thought Lombard looked pissed off as he stomped across the floor. She knew the feeling well enough. Dale had seen to that.

Lombard stopped ten feet from the outer edge of the two dozen kids gathered on the far end of the gym and put his hands on his hips. He kept his eyes on the floor as if disgusted with the bunch of them.

But when the P.E. teacher looked up, his eyes were wet and his cheeks were redder than Mandy had ever seen them. A cold stone dropped in Mandy's stomach, and she felt a stream of ice run down her back. Whatever Lombard was about to say was bad. Very bad.

Laurel nudged her, and Mandy made a small shrug.

Lombard sniffed. He looked back at the floor. "No class today," he said, his voice cracking on the last word, making it sound like *to-ay*. "Please get dressed and meet back here in twenty minutes. Mr. Thompkins has called a student assembly." Again his voice cracked.

"Oh, now, this cannot be good," Laurel said.

Mandy nodded and looked around at the other kids. They'd been dismissed, but no one moved. They stood just where they were standing when Lombard appeared, only now they looked confused, anxious, and disturbed. The P.E. teacher's distress had seeped into them, and her classmates did nothing to hide the fact. She continued searching each and every face.

It never occurred to her that one of them was missing.

Lake Crest was a small school, with fewer than three hundred students total. This year's graduating class would be just shy of one hundred. As a result, there were few strangers. Mandy had led or followed kids from Hoskins Elementary and Tyler Middle. She'd grown up in Elmwood, and whether she considered a kid her friend or not, they were all kind of close.

So when Mr. Thompkins cleared his throat and said, "I'm very sorry to have to announce the death of our friend Nicolette Marie Bennington," Mandy felt a deep sickness harden in her stomach. The nausea had been with her since Mr. Lombard had excused them. It had grown when she'd emerged from the girls' locker room to find the bleachers extended and her classmates gathering on the benches. The queasiness had been soft then, unformed and roiling like something she was trying to digest. But when their principal leaned forward at the podium, his voice oozing those words through the microphone, that soft undistinguished misery grew solid and sharp edged.

Beside her, both Laurel and Drew threw their hands over their faces. Sobbing. But Mandy couldn't do that. It was a joke. She didn't believe it. Just another one of Naughty Nic's silly jokes. Any minute, Nicki'd come dancing into the gym with a big smile. She'd say something like, "Who died?" and everyone would laugh, and her friends would stop crying. Everyone would stop crying.

"We will certainly miss Nicolette," continued Mr. Thompkins, wiping a handkerchief across his forehead. "For now, I would like you all to report to your homerooms. You will be excused from there. No one is to leave the school grounds alone. Those of you who need to arrange a ride with a family member may use the phone in the administration office. When you are excused, you are expected to return directly to your homes."

An arm snaked around her neck, startling Mandy. It was just Laurel, pulling her in to join her friends in an embrace. The three of them huddled together on the bench, hunched with heads touching. Entwined with Drew and Laurel, Mandy felt the sickness in her belly turn to an ache.

"This can't be true," she whispered.

She remembered things about Nicki, tiny things that she had no business remembering. Earlier that year, Nicki had worn a T-shirt to school that said Good Eats, and was sent home by Mrs. Fletcher, the biology teacher. The summer before, Mandy had seen Nicki in the park, lying in the shade of an oak reading an old book called *The Bell Jar*. Once she'd announced to the lunch line that the meatloaf was excellent because "They ground the cats coarse, so it's reeeeeal savory." Last Friday, she had worn a black sweater over a white blouse and earrings that looked like tiny thumbnail moons.

Then Mandy realized she would never see Nicki again, never laugh at one of her quick remarks. The sickness that had become an ache exploded and sent shattered bits of pain to every nerve in her body. She sobbed because her denial was gone. It was true. Naughty Nic was dead.

"How?" Mandy asked between sobs, pushing closer to Laurel, tightening her grasp on Drew.

How?

Speculation ran rampant in the homerooms of Lake Crest. It was Mr. Thompkins's fault, because he'd simply announced the death but given no indication of its cause. As a result, fertile minds blossomed with possibilities.

I'll bet she OD'd on crystal meth.

It wasn't an accident. No way. She killed herself. She was always talking about it.

She probably got hit by a car or something.

Maybe she slipped in the tub. That kills a lot of people.

Shut up, Brian. She didn't slip in the tub.

I think one of her boyfriends killed her. She hung out with a lot of Hannibals.

In Mrs. Fletcher's homeroom, Mandy, Laurel, and Drew also speculated. But they thought it less likely that Nic's death had been accidental. Through the window that looked out on Lake Crest Drive, they saw two police cars parked in the front lot. That told them Nicolette had not slipped in the tub or choked on a bit of chicken;

she had not stepped in front of a racing car. Every few minutes, Mr. Price, the assistant principal, would stick his head in the room and give a list of names to Mrs. Fletcher, who would then clear her throat and excuse another four students to follow Mr. Price to a different part of the building. The students must have gone home from there, because they didn't come back.

At the front of the room, Mrs. Fletcher, a woman with short gray hair jutting away from her face in ragged chunks, cleared her throat for the tenth time. She adjusted the collar on her blue blouse, scratched the back of her neck, and then returned to staring out the window, allowing the students to chat quietly.

"She could have killed herself," Drew said, her voice a high squeak. "The police would want to know if anything was bothering her. They'd ask us."

"No way," Laurel said, eyes shimmering with the remnants of tears. "They wouldn't come rolling in here like SWAT. They'd send a counselor or something. This is something else. Something bad."

"You don't know that," Mandy said, though she'd been thinking the same thing herself. "Let's just see what they tell us. It's probably . . ."

"Oh, this is some Megan's Law shit," Laurel piped in. "Nicki got herself snatched and buried. The freak probably licked her all over and chopped her into little bits and there's no way . . ."

"Stop it," Mandy said through a clenched jaw. "Just stop it. You don't know any more than we do."

Laurel's normally pretty face scrunched into an ugly mask, and she leaned back in her chair. "Whatever."

Mandy suddenly wished Dale was with her. Maybe she shouldn't have dissed him in the school parking lot. It wasn't an issue of forgiveness, just one of security. Usually, Dale drove her home from school. He played on the first-string football team. He was fast and strong, and though she didn't know if he would be a match for some psycho-perv, she suspected that a psycho-perv wasn't likely to reach into Dale's car and grab her. But no, the jerk had to cruise chat rooms, had to be a big shot for other girls. *Girls from our school!* God, how humiliating. She was angry at herself for thinking about him, especially now, but the idea that someone might be out there, just waiting for her to take a wrong step, chilled her.

"If they call you guys first, wait for me," Drew said, her voice trembling. "Okay?"

"My dad's already on his way," Laurel said. "He'll probably lock me in the house until I graduate or something."

Mandy looked out the window and saw two boys she recognized as sophomores walking past the police cars in the lot. One of the boys punched his friend's arm, and they both started laughing.

"Maybe it's not so bad," Mandy said, nodding toward the window.

Laurel and Drew turned their heads to see just as the classroom door opened. Mr. Price poked his head in, looked around as if to see if the coast was clear, and walked to Mrs. Fletcher's desk. He handed her a note, which she promptly unfolded. He turned to the class, tried to smile, but it was one of those phony smiles that looked like he had just stubbed his toe.

Mrs. Fletcher cleared her throat. The first name she read was Mandy's. That sick feeling returned to her stomach.

Laurel and Drew both stood up and hugged her tight.

"Wait for me?" Drew whispered anxiously.

"I'll wait," Mandy said, then gathered her books and joined Mr. Price. She waited until the other three students were called and came to the front of the room. Then Mr. Price opened the door and led them into the hall.

She was led down the hall toward the administration office. Ahead, Mr. Price marched authoritatively, though his head was down. Farther down the hall, another group of kids followed Mr. Thompkins. This group turned right at the school's lobby and disappeared, though when Mr. Price reached the lobby, he guided them across the shiny linoleum. When her foot came down on the face of Wally, the school mascot painted on the floor, another chill ran down Mandy's back. Wally was a shark with big eyes and a single row of pointed teeth. One of his fins was raised in a fist and the other tipped the sailor cap on his head. Mandy's foot came right down on his mouth, and the sight of her shoe floating between those sharp teeth unnerved her.

Mr. Price turned right at the end of the lobby and led the small group of kids toward the math classes. Outside the first door, a row of desks had been pushed against the wall.

"Mandy, come with me," Mr. Price said. "The rest of you have a seat. This won't take long."

She watched her classmates sit in the chairs, a knot of anxiety pulling tight in her stomach. Next to her, Mr. Price opened the door and swept his hand to usher Mandy over the threshold. The classroom was empty except for a plump woman in a blue uniform sitting behind the teacher's desk. A plastic chair faced the desk, and the woman extended her arm toward it, indicating that Mandy should take a seat.

"This is Mandy Collins," Mr. Price said. Then he turned to her. "Mandy, this is Officer Romero. She'd like to ask you a few questions."

"Okay."

Mr. Price left them alone, and Mandy looked at the woman, whose blocky body pushed against the too-tight fabric of her uniform. She had a pretty, darkly tanned face with large green eyes.

"There's no need to be nervous," Officer Romero said.

"I'm not," Mandy lied, feeling the jitters run through her like little electric currents. She sat down.

"This is very informal. If you're uncomfortable answering questions now, you can come down to the station with your parents later. We don't want to make this tragedy any harder on you than we have to."

"Okay."

"Now then, did you know Nicolette Bennington?"

"Yes. I mean, we weren't best friends or anything."

"But you knew her?"

"Yes."

"Did you ever see her outside of school?"

She thought about Nicolette in dark glasses holding Hamlet's leash standing in a Lady Foot Locker, thought about the girl lying under an oak tree fascinated by the book in her hands. But she said, "No, not really. We didn't hang out."

"Do you know who she did hang out with?"

"She kind of kept to herself. I mean, she was nice. Everybody liked her, but she just kind of kept to . . . I already said that. No."

"Did she ever mention a boyfriend?"

Mandy shook her head. The only time Nicki ever mentioned boys was in a joking way, like they were funny to her. Mandy couldn't remember if she'd ever dated any of the boys at Lake Crest.

"Okay," said Officer Romero. "This question is a little tougher, and I want you to really think about it. Have you noticed any strange men hanging around your school, maybe parked in a car or standing across the road?"

A nervous joke occurred to Mandy: *Aren't all men strange?* She mentally scolded herself for such an inappropriate thought. This was serious, and she had to treat it that way. So she put her mind to work, imagined all of the times she'd left the grounds after school. But Dale was in those thoughts, his arm looped around her neck as he walked Mandy to his car. She certainly didn't want to be thinking about Dale, but it was impossible not to. They always used to leave together. *Not anymore*, she thought.

She edited Dale out of her thoughts, concentrating on memories of the streets and yards and trees surrounding the campus. Nothing came to her.

"I'm sorry," she said finally. "I haven't."

"That's okay." The woman lifted a small business card from the desk and handed it to Mandy. "This is the number of the police station. You can call us anytime."

"Thank you," Mandy said, sliding the business

31

card into the pocket of her blouse. She stood and then blurted out the question that had been nagging her since the assembly. "What happened to Nicki, Officer Romero?"

The police officer's pretty face scrunched as if in pain. "It'll be on the news tonight," she said. "What I can tell you is that she was abducted from her home last night. The body was found a few hours later."

The body? Mandy thought in disbelief. How could she say that? It wasn't a body. It was a girl. A girl named Nicki. A girl she *knew*!

"Thanks," she whispered, and walked out of the room.

Mandy's room was a mess, or so her mother said. The rest of the house was spotless and shining, filled with glass and metal and marble. The only concessions to forestry were the hardwood floors throughout and a series of bookcases in her father's den, but even these were sanitized, the pine having been bleached near white. Everything beyond her bedroom door was modern and cold. Mandy just didn't like it, even though her friends thought the minimalist gleam was cool. In defiance of all things sleek, Mandy had a cherrywood bedroom suite with a matching computer desk. Her bed was covered in a thick fabric with an intricate print of swirling crimson, brown, and gold.

Last year, she had insisted that her mother buy her a deep red cotton rug to cover the floor, because the polished boards made her think of a bowling alley. While her mother kept all the glass and stone tabletops clear, save for the well-placed bronze or crystal knick-knack and silver picture frame, Mandy used the surfaces in her room. Books and magazines, CDs and DVDs, school papers and pictures of her friends were everywhere: on her desk, on her chest of drawers, stacked in neat piles on the floor.

"We can have cabinets built in for all of that," her mother once said.

Mandy had rolled her eyes and asked her mother to leave.

Though she loved her room, even Mandy had to admit that it was dark that afternoon. The curtains were open, and sunlight poured through. It didn't matter. The room *felt* dark, and Mandy imagined she could be on a sun-drenched beach, and she'd still think it gloomy.

On the bed, Drew flipped through an issue of *Teen People*, not really reading, barely gazing at the pictures. Mandy could tell that her friend was just looking for a distraction from the morning's bad news. They'd talked all the way home, and this was a quiet pause, a moment for the batteries to recharge.

Poor Drew, Mandy thought. She was always a little scared of the world, though Mandy didn't know why. Boys absolutely terrified her, and even before this terrible business with Nicki, Drew had hated being alone.

Mandy sat at her computer. She had done a Google search to see if Nicki was on the news yet, but the only mentions said little more than Officer Romero had. Girl abducted. Body found. She checked e-mail and, except for a note from Laurel—*Yeah, Daddy's flippin'. See you next decade.*—her mailbox was empty. *Strange,* she thought. She'd expected to have dozens of e-mails from friends wanting to discuss Nicki, her death, and the cops at school. Mandy thought they should all be talking about this, yet even she couldn't think of who to write to or what to put in a note.

It was all just so weird. This was the kind of thing you saw on the news, like the Middle East. It was something distant, something you understood in the way you understood the moon. Murder existed. It was there. But you never expected it to come close to you.

Behind her, the television was on. She kept her ears alert, waiting for some news about Nicki, but the big city stations probably wouldn't run the story until five. That was hours away.

"Do you think it was someone from school?" Drew asked, dropping the magazine on the bed. "I mean, do you think anyone here could have done this?"

Mandy didn't know. It should have been impossible to believe—these were people she'd known for years—but the idea was with her now. Maybe freaky Derek with the big ears and the biker jacket had finally snapped, no longer satisfied to just get high and listen to Nu-metal. Peter Harris or Ned Schwartz could have done it. They were so obsessed with video games and horror movies—they'd totally be suspects. It could have been a teacher. Not someone like Mr. Lombard or Mr. Stahlman, who taught English, but Mandy certainly wouldn't put it past Mr. Grohl: even as shop teachers went, he was pretty skeezy. It could have been a woman, she reasoned. After all, no one had said how Nicki was killed. But all of this was silly. These were her friends and her teachers.

"I don't know," she said. "I guess. I just wish they'd tell us something."

"I know!" Drew said too loudly. She leaned forward on the bed, her eyes wide. "It's like the worst part because we don't know anything. I mean, was it a drifter? Or like maybe her family? Or a boyfriend or something? It's like they won't tell me who to be afraid of, so I'm afraid of everyone."

That wasn't exactly new territory for Drew, but Mandy knew what she meant. Without some idea about the cause or the killer, there wasn't much to hold on to in the way of comfort.

"God, it could be *anyone*," Drew said with more than enough drama to exasperate Mandy.

She was about to say something logical, like *It couldn't be our parents or your brothers or Laurel*, just to contradict Drew's über-paranoia and keep her from bursting into tears again, but her cell phone trilled. Drew leaped off the bed with a yelp. Her hand fanning the air in front of her face like she was trying to get rid of a bad smell, Drew danced from foot to foot.

"Oh my God! That scared me so bad."

"You need a pill," Mandy said, sliding over the bed to grab her phone from the nightstand. She checked the caller ID to make sure Dale wasn't getting his stalker on and saw that the name was blocked. Not Dale. His name came through bright and shiny whenever he called.

"Girl, where are you?" Laurel asked before Mandy finished saying hello.

"I'm at home, where we're all supposed to be. Where are you?"

"I'm in the chat with, like, *everyone*."

Of course, Mandy thought. That was why her mailbox wasn't choking on e-mails. Everyone she knew was logged in to one of the school chat rooms. There were two: one that was actually moderated by school staff, and one that was independent of the Lake Crest website, which was the best place to learn about parties and anything else parents and teachers weren't supposed to know about.

"Official or un?" Mandy asked.

"Please," Laurel said. "Only bottom-feeders use the official site. Now log on. Is Drew with you?"

"Yeah."

"Well, slide your butts to the screen. I've never seen this place bangin' so hard."

And Laurel was right. More than thirty kids had logged in to the room. Mandy told Drew to slide the bench at the end of her bed over so she could see. Once she had, they both scanned the usernames and found they recognized all of them.

"Jacob's signed on," Drew said, all but gushing the name of the boy she'd been crushing on for the last two years.

"Still needing that pill," Mandy said, bumping Drew with her shoulder.

"What are they saying?"

The truth was, Mandy couldn't tell. Lines of text were rolling up the screen so fast she couldn't keep up with it all. She saw variations of Nicolette's name—Nicki and Naughty Nic—and words like *murdered*, *stabbed*, *shotgun*, but just as her eyes would lock on to a line, it was gone.

"It's like they just want to get it all out," Mandy said. "They don't care if anyone can read it or not."

"Say hi to Jacob."

"Not."

"What did that line say? Something about her being raped? Oh God. She was raped!"

"They don't know, Drew. Calm down. None of us knows anything yet."

An IM window opened on the screen; it was from Laurel.

Laurel2good4u: Do I speak truth or what?

MC9010025: This is crzy

Laurel2good4u: Best Beleev. U going 2 vigil 2nite

MC9010025: ???

Laurel2good4u: Candlelight vigil 4 Nic. Elmwood Park. 7

"I'm not going out in the dark," Drew exclaimed right into Mandy's ear. "Are they crazy? Why don't they just hand us over to the guy with a chainsaw and say 'Happy birthday, Chucky'?"

"There are going to be a billion people there, Drew."

MC9010025: R U?

Laurel2good4u: Y. But dad's taggin. Meet by fountain?

MC9010025: Y

Laurel2good4u: Kewl. TTFN dads freakin AGAIN. I'm out

MC9010025: TTFN

Mandy closed the window, returning her attention to the rolling lines of text filling the chat room. She decided to scroll to the top and read what had come in since signing on; she'd never be able to keep up with the new comments. But as she read through, she discovered that her first feeling had been right. Her friends were just venting. They shared their fondest memories about Nicolette.

She kissed me on the nose and said "Nope, no prince."

She told my mom that donuts were pure carbs, and when Mom said she had a fast metabolism, N said that apparently her metabolism hadn't let her ass in on that information.

She designed fliers for me when my cat got lost.

She danced with me at the junior prom.

She walked me home when that a**hole Joe dumped me.

She always smiled.

I really, really, really miss her already.

Scattered among these reminiscences were speculations about Nicki's fate. Only now, no one believed the cause of her death was accidental.

And of course, amid all of the fond memories and the wondering were fear and anger. *If I catch that SOB, I'm going to tear his head off. They ought to open him up and fill him with scorpions, drag behind my car, needles in his eyes, baseball bat to the nuts.* Over two dozen variations on these could be found, though it was unanimously agreed that anything they could come up with was "too good for the bastard."

"Oh God, look what Jacob said."

Mandy scrolled back, looking for Jacob Lurie's screen handle and the message beside it. When she found it, she groaned and shook her head.

I'd pound his face.

"He would too," Drew assured her.

"Jacob weighs like fifty pounds."

"He's wiry."

"In this case *wiry* means *toast*." Mandy ignored Drew's whining protest. "There's nothing here. They're all just guessing."

A new IM window opened. Mandy's heart clenched when she saw Dale's username. Very aware of Drew's presence at her back, Mandy kept it cool. Neither Drew nor Dale needed to know how upset she was.

DaleLineBacker90: R U OK? Worried about U

"I bet," Mandy said. Part of her wanted to write, *U seemed more worried about other girls last night*. Or maybe something simple like *Whatever*. Instead, she just closed the window.

"You should answer him," Drew said. "We're all pretty freaked."

"So?" Mandy asked.

"I just thought . . ." Drew let the sentence die on her lips.

"Let me recap," Mandy said. "The dumbass was flirting with some girl in a chat room. He invited her to his house to watch DVDs, and he didn't even bother closing the IM window so I wouldn't see it. So, he is either astronomically stupid or he let me see it to be mean. Neither of these things is high on my list of coolicious boyfriend traits. Now he thinks that I'm going to let him talk me out of dumping him because something terrible happened, and that brings us right back to astronomically stupid."

"Okay," Drew said. "God. Who needs a pill now?"

"Everyone," Mandy said in frustration. "They can hand them out at the vigil tonight."

"Are you really going?"

"Yes," she said. "And you should too. Nicki was one of us."

"They'll have a funeral," Drew said quietly.

"It's not the same. The funeral is to say good-bye. This is to show how much she meant to us."

Drew nodded, her eyes now soft with understanding. Then, she pointed a finger at the computer screen over Mandy's shoulder.

Mandy turned to find another IM window open. No tone had sounded to alert her, or at least she hadn't heard one, but there was the window. At first she figured it was just Dale with another stupid message, but she quickly saw that the screen handle was not familiar.

Kylenevers: Hey

"Who the hell is this?" Mandy said aloud.

Drew pushed in close to look over her shoulder. "Somebody named Kyle?"

"Well, that clears everything up," Mandy said. "Do you know him?"

"No. I mean, not unless it's Kyle from biology class."

"This isn't his username."

"Say hi."

Mandy shrugged.

MC9010025: Hi
Kylenevers: Kewl profile.
MC9010025: Thnx. Do I know U?
Kylenevers: Probably not.

"Check his profile," Drew said. "He might be hot."

"Have you ever met anyone who put 'hideously deformed' in their profile?" Mandy asked.

"Well, he might have loaded a picture."

"I'm just not caring right now. He's probably some looz surfing keywords or something."

MC9010025: This isn't really a good time.
Kylenevers: Oh sorry. Take it easy. BFN
MC9010025: U 2

Mandy closed the window.

"I'll bet he was hot," Drew said. She stood from the dressing bench and returned to the bed, where she dropped down hard on the covers. When she stopped bouncing on the mattress, she rolled onto her back. "What if he was like this absolutely perfect guy? And it was fate that he messaged you, and now you'll never know because you deleted him, and he's gone forever?"

"Happens all the time." Mandy clicked on her away message so she didn't have to deal with any more instant messages. "I'll have to find some way to live with it."

Mandy's mother returned home from work an hour early. She didn't usually get home until six, but Mandy heard the key in the lock, startling Drew into another yelp. Mrs. Collins walked into the den, where the girls were waiting for the news to come on, and put her handbag down on the edge of the glass-topped, lacquered cabinet. The act was unheard of in the Collins household. That glass top was reserved for a family portrait secured in a crystal frame and a large black crystal bear. Nothing else touched its surface. Ever. Her mother had to be really upset. It didn't show in her face, though.

"Hello, Drew," Mandy's mother said, running a hand through her blond hair. She crossed the den, threw a glance at the cocktail table—a reflex, Mandy knew, checking to make sure the girls were using coasters for their coffee mugs—and leaned down to kiss Mandy's cheek. "How are you?"

"Fine."

Mrs. Collins's lips twisted into a tight smile and her eyes grew doe soft, like she was looking at Mandy after a successful operation: concern, relief, and pity mingled in her expression. "Are you?" she asked, a bit too seriously.

"Yes, Mom," Mandy said. Normally she would have added a *Jeez, chill out*, but this wasn't the time for attitude. Her mom was worried and Mandy got that. "We came back here after school."

"Has there been any news?" Mrs. Collins asked.

"It's just coming on."

"Drew," Mandy's mom said, "does your father know you're here?"

"Yes, Mrs. Collins," Drew said quietly. "My father knows. He'll be home at five-thirty."

"Well, good."

Mandy watched her mother's uncomfortable hovering. Clearly, she didn't know what else to say and had no fresh excuse to remain with the girls, but she didn't want to leave. Her worry warmed Mandy; it made her feel a little awkward, but good.

"You can watch the news with us if you want," Mandy said, sliding closer to Drew on the sofa to make room for her mother to sit. "It's coming on now."

"Maybe I will," Mrs. Collins said, lowering herself to the cushion.

The three settled in and Mandy retrieved her mug from the table, holding it to her lips. The flashing graphics of the local news program came on. Drew pushed closer, her leg bouncing nervously against Mandy's.

"Another car bomb rocks the Iraqi capital," the African American anchor with the thick mustache said. "And, is Britney Spears pregnant again? These stories coming up, but first, tragedy strikes a local youth. . . ."

"Oh," Drew moaned tearfully.

A picture of Nicki suddenly appeared to the right of the anchorman. Her black hair hung to her shoulders in a neat wave; her eyes sparkled. From the mottled blue background, Mandy could tell it was a yearbook photo.

She's so pretty, Mandy thought. *And she's dead.* A fist of sadness punched her belly.

The picture of Nicki disappeared, replaced by a video showing the corner of a blond brick building, a field of tall, brown grass, and a stand of trees beyond. "That's the library," Mrs. Collins said, practically sighing out the words. A half dozen men, some in police uniforms, some in suits, and one in a white smock coat, walked through the dry grass, looking intently at the ground.

The anchorman's voice accompanied the images.

"This morning at about three a.m., police found the remains of seventeen-year-old Nicolette Bennington in a wooded area behind Elmwood Public Library. Bennington, a Lake Crest High senior, was abducted from her home last night by an unknown assailant."

A thin-faced man with gray hair appeared on the screen, standing in front of the library. The man was the chief of Elmwood's police department. Beside him, a woman in a police uniform stood with her hands clasped behind her back. A flash of recognition struck Mandy as Officer Romero looked up at the camera. The policewoman looked just as serious and as concerned as she had when speaking to Mandy that morning. Her eyes were sad, but her jaw was set with determination as she listened to her boss speak.

"Our hearts go out to the Bennington family," said Police Chief Dean. "At this time, we're combing the area for forensic evidence. No suspects or persons of interest have been currently identified, but we're following a number of leads. We know that we'll bring Nicolette's killer to justice soon. That's all we have at this time."

"Nicolette's parents had no comment for us, but local residents are in a state of shock," the anchor continued.

Another familiar face appeared on the screen. Tracy Renquist, a girl who shared the same P.E. class as Mandy, Laurel, and Nicolette, hugged herself tightly. She stood in front of Lake Crest High, eyes red from crying.

"My God, that's Tracy," Drew announced. "She's in my English and Poli-Sci classes. We went to camp together."

"It's horrible," Tracy cried into a microphone. "Nicki was just so great. I can't believe this."

"When were they at school?" Mandy asked. She hadn't seen any news vans when leaving the school grounds.

"They must have come after we left," Drew said. "Look, there's Mr. Thompkins, and, oh my God, Dale."

"My eyes work," Mandy said. As Mr. Thompkins expressed his condolences to Nicki's family, behind him, on the steps of the school, Dale stared at the walk, looking dazed and sad. Seeing him tugged at Mandy's chest. She wanted to be with him. He'd hold her close and make some of the sadness and fear go away.

Why did the jerk have to pick last night to pull such a lame stunt?

After the report ended and the anchorman turned his attention to Iraq, Drew was crying again. Mandy's eyes stung, but she didn't break down. Instead, she held Drew. Her mother patted her leg, then excused herself.

"I'll fix some dinner, so we can make it to the park by seven."

Apparently, her mother already knew about the candlelight vigil.

Mandy looked around the crowd, over her shoulder at the fountain, and into the dark band of trees on the far end of the lawn. She stood with her mother at the north end of the park in Holm Field, an expanse of grass roughly half the size of a football field. In the center of the lawn was a landscaped garden with concrete walks winding between plots of dirt that come spring would be bursting with flowers. The fountain was the focal point of the garden. An ornate concrete sculpture stood twice Mandy's height. People holding candles surrounded them and formed a rough fan shape facing north, where a small platform had been erected. Next to the platform, Mandy could just make out the sorrow-creased faces of Mr. and Mrs. Bennington; Nicolette's older brother, Stan; and a group of people Mandy imagined were family and close friends. Between her and them, the flames of hundreds of candles cast an orange glow over the people and the field.

Oddly, Mandy thought about Elton John. She didn't want to, but there he was in her head.

When she was a little girl, only six years old, her parents brought her with them to an Elton John concert in the city. She remembered being hoisted onto her father's shoulders and looking out over a sea of shadows, dappled with flickering flames. Fans held lighters in the air, tiny bits of light, like stars, in the dark arena. Her dad bounced her with excitement, and she was entranced by the tiny sky rolling out before her. When she looked down, she saw her mother's face bathed in the dancing flame of a lighter. Then, Elton John was there, pounding on piano keys.

She remembered little else about the concert, but she remembered the thrill and the good feeling and her mother glowing with warm light. There was no thrill for Mandy tonight, standing in the park. But there was her mother, face awash in candlelight.

"So many people," Mrs. Collins said, tipping her candle to let wax drip into the paper collar, protecting her hand. "Are Drew and Laurel coming?"

"Supposed to."

"Their parents were probably driving them in, and I can't imagine parking being easy. It looks like the entire town is here."

Just as her mother finished speaking, Laurel appeared at the edge of the crowd. Barely a foot behind her, hovering like her shadow, was Laurel's father, his face stern and dangerous looking. He searched the crowd anxiously, eyes darting from side to side.

"Girl, get this damned bodyguard off my back," Laurel whispered in Mandy's ear while they hugged.

Mandy laughed and squeezed tight before stepping away. "Can't help you with that."

"He's been on me like a rash since I got home from school. He took the rest of the week off. God, even *we* have to go to school Friday."

"He's worried about you."

"Ya think?" Laurel looked around and said hi to Mandy's mother. She waved at her own father, who stood less than four feet away, mocking his concern playfully. "Where's the Drew?"

"Don't know. She was pretty weirded about being out past dark."

"Figures. She thinks the shadows have teeth. Dale and his posse are over by the benches."

"So?" Mandy asked sharply.

"Just sayin'."

"Well, don't. That's the last thing I need tonight."

At the front of the crowd a whine of feedback sounded. Mandy looked up to see Mr. Bennington pulling away from the microphone. He looked around confused for a moment, then leaned forward to speak.

"Here we go," Laurel said, looping her arm around Mandy's.

By the time Mr. Bennington thanked everyone and shared a few words about his daughter, and Nicki's brother, Stan, made an impassioned plea for justice, Mandy was tired and cold. She had shed a lot of tears that day. She just wanted to sleep and maybe even forget, though she knew that wasn't going to happen.

Drew showed up with her father just as the formal presentation ended.

"Dad didn't want to come," Drew said. "I mean,

I didn't *want* to come, but I knew I *had* to, you know, for Nicki."

The three walked a bit farther away from their parents to the back edge of the fountain. Laurel's father gave them a hard glare, looked at the grassy field behind them, and then returned his attention to the platform, where Nicolette's aunt walked up to the microphone.

"So, y'all have to come over tomorrow," Laurel said, once she was certain her father couldn't hear them. "I'm in lockdown, and I'll go full-on Mariah if I have to sit around there by myself with Daddy pacing outside my door."

"Okay," Mandy said, not sure if her parents had plans to work the next day or not.

"Totally," Drew said. "I'm not staying at my place by myself, and my dad is acting like it's no big deal."

"Cool," Laurel said. "Somebody bring DVDs. Something funny. We've got enough drama these days. Nothing with David Spade, though. I hate that guy."

"Who doesn't?" Mandy asked.

They stood quietly for a few moments as Nicolette's aunt finished a poem about clocks stopping. Mandy checked her mom, who was looking at the stage, so she only saw her back. Laurel's dad looked at them again, and Drew's dad checked his watch before doing a quick survey of the crowd.

"What do you think Nicki wanted to do after high school?" Drew asked, suddenly.

Both Mandy and Laurel looked at her like she'd just sprouted warts and a tail.

"*What?*" Drew asked. "We know who she was, but we don't know who she would have been. That's what was lost. I mean, did she want to go to college? Did she want to be a mother? She could have formed a rock group or become president. She could have become anything she wanted. I can't stop thinking about that."

"A vet," Laurel said. "We talked about it once, and she wanted to be a vet. She loved animals. She didn't have a question in her mind about it. Nicki would have been a veterinarian."

"She's going to miss so much," Drew said, welling up with tears.

"Yeah, she is, but you don't have to make it sound like it's her fault," Mandy said. "Jeez, Drew, grow some tact."

"That's not what I meant."

"Whatever," Laurel said.

"But, I mean, what if she did do something? I mean, something like this doesn't just happen, right? I'm not saying she did anything wrong, just did something. Maybe she broke up with the guy or made fun of him. She was always making fun of people. Maybe she was teasing him, leading him on. I don't know, something."

"I have never wanted to call someone 'bitch' so much in my life," Laurel said.

"Calm down, L," Mandy said. "She's just trying to make sense of this."

"There is no sense in this," Laurel said, growing angrier. "This is life, not some fairy tale. Psychos aren't interested in morality plays. They hunt and they slice and it's usually the innocent that take the blade. So put all of your Brothers Grimm she-had-it-comin' crap away. The only thing Nicki did was *not* plant a boot in this guy's sac and run fast enough to get away from him. And if you think being all innocent and sweet is gonna protect you from anything, then take a good look around, because the next one of these is yours."

Mandy looked on, astonished. Drew burst into tears, her hands covering her face, shoulders trembling.

"Think you could be a little more Simon?" Mandy asked.

Laurel folded her arms across her chest in defiance. Mandy looked at Drew, who kept her face buried in her hands, and shook her head.

"Great," Mandy said. She walked over and pulled Drew into a hug. Her friend sobbed harder and pushed in tight to her side.

Then Mandy's cell phone vibrated in her jacket pocket, and she had to pull away. She looked at the device, saw that she had a text message, considered ignoring it, but was eager for a distraction. Right now, anything was better than dealing with the drama. She opened the phone and retrieved the message.

When she saw the letters printed across the tiny screen, they confused her. She squinted as if the act might bring clarity, but there were only two letters, repeated over and over. They were perfectly clear, but they made no sense. Unless someone had a very sick sense of humor. A profound chill, so strong that it made her tremble, ran over her neck as she read:

Hahahahahahahaha.

"I still think Dale sent that text," Laurel said, curling her legs under her on the overstuffed chair in her bedroom. She dropped the remote in her lap and reached for the glass of tea she'd set on the windowsill.

"Why would he?" Drew asked from her place on the bed.

The two had forged a functioning truce since Nicki's vigil the night before. Mandy imagined it was more a result of Drew's fear of being left home alone than any real forgiveness, but it was a start. Now the three of them sat in Laurel's bedroom. An Ashton Kutcher DVD was paused on the television screen.

"To freak her out," Laurel said. "He gets her all

scared with this whack job running around, and she comes running back to his big strong arms."

"Oh," Drew said, as if that made perfect sense.

"It's not Dale," Mandy said. "He's not into subtle. Last night he left three voice messages on my cell. Besides, even if he were able to think of a scheme like that, which I'm finding highly doubtful, I don't think he's sick enough to do it. I mean, the message was basically laughing at Nicki's death, unless I'm totally missing something. He may be an ass, but I don't think he's that deep down cruel."

"He let you catch him sniffing around the chat easy enough."

That was true. Maybe Dale was sick, like really twisted. It happened all the time. The guys that seemed to be so together were often just good at hiding something foul and dark. And someone like Dale, a privileged brat who apparently had no morals, could certainly work up that kind of nastiness. *No*, she thought. *You're just angry at him.* Dale wasn't a freak. He was a guy—just a big, stupid guy. He wasn't evil.

"How would he block his user ID? I mean the text message came through without a handle. Dale couldn't have figured out how to do that. He can't even program his cell phone."

Laurel smiled broadly and put her tea back on the windowsill. "Maybe not, but he also can't figure out geometry, which is why he has geek-king Matthew do it for him. Are you seeing my ever-so-subtle point?"

"I didn't even know you could hide your ID like that," Drew said.

"Well, it happened, which means it can be done." This from Laurel. "I'm the Goddess of Tech, but they come out with functions and features so fast that even I can't keep up."

"So," Mandy said, "you think Dale had Matt do this for him?"

"I'm just saying it's one big, obvious, really likely possibility."

"God, that's so romantic," said Drew.

Laurel slowly turned her head toward Drew on the bed, then looked at Mandy. "You are going to let me slap her, right?"

"Well, he's doing all of this for Mandy," Drew said. "Just to get her back. I mean he's obviously thinking about her a lot."

"Logic fault," Mandy said. "If he had spent ten seconds thinking about me—the ten he spent writing 'kewl profile, let me grab your tits' to that girl online—none of this would be an issue."

Laurel laughed and clapped her hands. "Girl's got the right head on this one."

"I just think it's cool to have someone missing you that way."

"And yet so many stalker victims still press charges," Mandy said. "Look, whatever. It's over. If it was him, his plan didn't work. If it wasn't . . ."

Mandy didn't know how to finish that statement. She didn't have to. As she was speaking, Laurel's door burst open and her father shoved his head in the room. Drew, naturally, yelped and fanned her face, and Laurel opened her mouth to protest, but her father was already talking.

"Turn on the news," he said, stomping into the room, heading directly for the television. "They have a picture of the guy. You all need to see this, need to know what to look out for. Why is the screen frozen? Who is this? What's wrong with this television set?"

Laurel pulled the remote from her lap and hit a button, sending Ashton Kutcher's face away and replacing him with an episode of *Saturday Night Live*. "What channel?" she asked.

"Try four."

Laurel pressed a button. The three girls gathered on the bed for the best view of the screen. A grainy black-and-white picture hung frozen above the anchorman's shoulder. Then it came to life, showing a hunched man in a black coat pulling someone across what looked like a parking lot. The angle was odd; it seemed to be shot from high up. The man was looking over his shoulder, giving the camera a blurry profile. The person with him yanked hard, trying to escape. He yanked back, and all of them gasped when Nicolette Bennington's frightened face came into the frame.

"Where's the volume?" Laurel's father asked.

Laurel hit a button.

"Again, police are looking for this man in connection with the abduction and murder of Nicolette Bennington."

"Damn," Laurel's dad said angrily. "That didn't give you a good enough look. If you kids were paying attention and actually took this seriously instead of just watching your little heartthrobs telling fart jokes . . ."

"Dad! Breathe! We'll download it off the Web."

Her father looked at her like she'd just slapped

him. Confusion and anger took turns scrunching his features. With no reply, he simply shook his head and walked out of the room.

The best picture they could find, the one that showed the most of the man's face, filled Laurel's computer screen less than two minutes later. The image was black-and-white, taken by a security camera concealed in the eaves of the library. It showed the large, stooped man in a long black coat, his hand firmly grasping Nicki's bicep. He looked feral, like an animal.

"God, Nicki must have been so scared," Drew said.

Yes, Mandy thought. She was scared herself, and she was only looking at a bad picture of the man. She wasn't being held by him, dragged into the dark woods at the back of the library where he would . . .

"He's like grandpa old," Laurel said. "Total Crypt Keeper."

She had that right. From the side, the man's nose was rounded like a beak over his thin lips. His chin seemed to point downward, but Mandy thought that might just be a trick of the shadows or maybe a beard that had lost definition in the photograph. The eye she could see was surrounded by puffy flesh. His eyebrows rested on a pronounced ridge. His cheek sank into shadow just above his jaw. Mandy thought about the images of witches she'd seen in elementary school. He reminded her of those, only male, without the hat and broom, and very real.

"Gotta be a drifter," Laurel announced. "They would have caught him already if he was local. You can't hide a face like that."

Though disturbed by the image, Mandy found herself relieved. Nicki's killer had not been one of them, had not been a friend or acquaintance— *she'd never hang out with someone like that—* and this knowledge was soothing in its own way. She felt safer.

"At least we know who to look out for," Drew said. "God, he's so creepy."

"Yes, he is," Laurel agreed. "I think we need some Ashton to wash that freak out of our eyes."

Mandy left Drew at Laurel's house, hoping her friends would talk and put last night's misunderstanding behind them for good. Walking through the cool afternoon air, she felt uneasy. She lived in the same neighborhood as Laurel, only seven blocks away, and though she never once saw anyone creeping through yards, the terrible man from the news followed her home. She kept throwing looks over her shoulder and to the sides, checking the narrow yards that ran beside familiar houses. She carried him in her head, his beak nose, his thin lips. The thought of his fingers made her skin crawl.

Her feet moved faster as she told herself that he had moved on. He couldn't stay anywhere in town—in the state—without being recognized. His face was all over the news. His face, his nose, his lips, his fingers . . .

Don't run, she told herself. *Just be cool. There's no way he's out here. Don't freak.* Walking up her own driveway, Mandy tingled with anxiety. She didn't want to be alone in the house. Once inside, she locked the door with trembling fingers, then hurried to the kitchen to test the back door locks as well. Upstairs, checking e-mail, she did not turn on music, but instead listened for any break in the house's quiet.

Again, she was surprised by how few e-mails waited in her inbox. Half a dozen friends she'd seen at the vigil dropped notes, commenting on the sad event. Dale wrote her two notes, both of which she erased on sight. The ritual of e-mail comforted her. There was spam from an online clothing store where she'd bought a blouse once, an offer to buy Viagra online, and a note from a screen handle she didn't immediately recognize.

Kylenevers
Subject: Me Again
Hey, sorry about yesterday. I know we don't know each other. Kyle here. I feel kind of bad about IMing you like that. With everything going on with N., I just wanted to chat . . . don't know a lot of people and was kind of upset. Going to the vigil last night helped. A really nice cere-mony. Were you there? Anyway, sorry. Maybe we can chat some other time. I really did like your profile. ;–) C ya.
K

"Not needing a looz for my buddy list," Mandy said. She closed the e-mail and was navigating the cursor to the delete button when the doorbell rang.

The sound was so unexpected, her heart leaped into her throat. She stood, left the desk, and creeped to the window. Doing her best to look without being seen, she searched the curb, then looked down at her driveway.

"Oh, perfect," she whispered, seeing Dale's silver Audi parked on the white concrete.

The doorbell rang again. Mandy considered ignoring it, like she had ignored his phone calls and his e-mails, but told herself she was being childish. This wasn't the mature way to handle a relationship. Not that being mature was one of Dale's strong points. Still, she knew that if she didn't talk to him, he'd keep coming around. Besides, if he was playing stupid jokes, like sending her twisted text messages, she wanted to put a stop to it. Right now.

At the front door, she looked through the window and saw Dale bouncing on his heels nervously. She hated to admit it, but he looked great, wearing a thin black leather jacket over a cream-colored sweater and perfectly faded jeans. His black hair was properly mussed and fixed with product. To her, he looked like a young Keanu Reeves. In fact, that's what most people thought. Mandy reached up to pat down her hair, then stopped in defiance.

She didn't care what she looked like, not for Dale. This wasn't a date!

Mandy opened the door, consciously drawing a frown on her lips. "Dale," she said dryly, as if already completely bored with the conversation, though her heart beat fast.

"Hey," he said, still fidgeting with nervous energy. "You okay?"

"I'm fine," she said coolly.

"Yeah, good. Look, you didn't return any of my messages or anything, and I was getting kind of worried. Things are kind of weird now with Nicki and all."

"I'm a big girl," Mandy told him. "I can take care of myself."

"Sure, yeah, I know," he said. "It's just, well, I was worried."

"You said that."

"I know," Dale replied, his voice shaky. He bounced on his heels again, looked over his shoulder at the street and the houses, looked back at Mandy. "Could I come in? I mean, so we can talk?"

"Dale, I've said all I intend to." She liked the confident sound of her voice. It was strong and in control. This was the way she had sounded in her head, when she'd imagined all the things she would say to him. "We obviously have very different ideas about what a relationship is."

"Come on, Mandy. No, we don't. I was just flirting, being stupid. It's no big deal. Nothing happened."

"Well, Dale, something did happen. You got caught. Besides that, you humiliated me, and now I have to deal with that, and so do you."

She could see him struggling for a comeback. He was trapped. She didn't know if he was going to go the childish route and get angry with her, make some nasty comment, or if he was going to continue trying to talk his way out of it. When he did speak, he actually surprised her.

"You're right," he said. "I was stupid, too stupid to even know why I did it. But all of this stuff with Nicki is really getting to me. You know, making me think? About you and me and other stuff?"

Mandy's heart warmed. He looked so sad. She actually felt sorry for Dale, even after everything he'd done. But for all she knew, this was just another trick, another game. Part of her wanted to hold him and kiss him and pretend she'd never seen the instant message. Another part of her, the intelligent part, wanted to remain strong. Maybe they could work things out, but not until she knew for certain Dale was sincere.

"We've all been thinking a lot," she said. "I can't believe Nicki's gone, and it scares me, but I'm not going to use that as an excuse for us to get back together."

"I'm not saying that. I'm just saying that things are different now. God, you never listen to me." Anger was creeping into Dale's voice. He wasn't getting what he wanted, and since that was such a rare thing for Dale, he didn't know how to deal with it.

"You should go," Mandy said. "We can talk later."

"I want to talk now," he said.

"I don't."

"Why is it always about what you want?" he asked, the anger now clear. "It's not always about you. I mean, you just show up at my house and spy on what I'm doing. Then you freak out, and you don't even let me explain."

"I believe your explanation was 'Guys and girls are different.'"

"Well, they are," Dale said, reverting back to his

original argument. "I was just messing around. It didn't mean anything to me, but to you it's like some relationship nine-eleven."

"Bye, Dale," she said and closed the door. She threw the lock quickly and felt his fist hit the door through the handle.

Mandy leaped back, heard him shout, "God!" in frustration, then ran up the stairs, ignoring the ringing doorbell. He must have jabbed the button a dozen times before finally giving up.

In her room, Mandy sat on the edge of the bed, staring at the window. Her nerves were dancing on coals. That sick feeling took hold in her stomach again, and she gnawed on her thumb. Only when she heard Dale start his car and back out of the drive did she relax, and then just a little.

Mandy fell back on the bed and stared at the ceiling. She replayed their conversation in her head, always pausing at the moment he went from hurt to angry, wondering why his attitude changed so quickly. Maybe it was just hormones, like they talked about in Human Development class. She didn't know, but it worried her. Would it always be like this? Were all guys like this? Even adults? Boy, she hoped not.

A tone from her computer announced she had new mail, but Mandy wasn't interested. When her cell phone buzzed a few minutes later, she let it. She didn't want to think about Dale, or Nicki, or her killer. In fact, she just wanted a few minutes of peace. No boyfriend. No tragedy. No monsters. No typing on a keyboard or talking into a microphone, having to think of clever things to say. She couldn't remember the last time she just let herself zone out, ignoring messages inside and outside her head. She didn't know if she could do it, but she was going to try.

Her experiment in mental deprivation did not go well. Mandy lay on her bed, stared at the ceiling, tried any number of tricks to block out Dale, Nicki, Laurel, Drew, and a man she thought resembled a cartoon witch. Instead of blocking them out, her mind jumbled them, and she went into a kind of daydream. Then, she fell asleep, and solid, true dreams took hold of her mind.

Dale and the Witchman sat together in the school cafeteria, joking and shaking their heads, talking about Mandy, she knew. The Witchman extended a long finger that looked like a scalpel and poked at the air. This made Dale double over with laughter, while the Witchman threw his hands up, miming the protests of a screaming victim.

Next to her, Drew said, "God, it's so romantic. I mean, to have them thinking about you all the time." Laurel nudged her shoulder. When Mandy turned to look at her friend, Laurel shook her head solemnly. Where her eyes should have been were empty black sockets. She held candles in both palms, and the wax dripped over her hands, sealing them in bumpy white gloves.

The cafeteria was gone. Behind Laurel, whose head continued to turn from side to side, stood a blond brick building, the library. It was night, and the floodlights bathed the edge of the parking lot in a dull amber glow. Beyond the light, a field of tall dead grass ran to a stand of black woods. The trees looked like they were moving, but then Mandy's eyes adjusted, and she saw them:

A hundred people—men and women, boys and girls—seemed to be carved from smoke. They sat at similarly misty desks, typing frantically at computer keyboards, staring vacantly at panel screens made of fog. Two girls paced back and forth at the tree line, cell phones growing from their heads like tumors. They did not speak into the phones, simply listened, shambling back and forth between the trees.

Nicki was there, walking through the field of dead grass. Her steps were jerky and slow, and each one seemed to hurt her a little more. As she approached Mandy, she became less mist and more flesh, growing more solid with each agonizing step.

Mandy's heart raced; her pulse thundered in her ears. Nicki was coming to give her a message. Mandy knew this, but didn't want to hear what the dead girl would say. The thought of Nicki's wisdom terrified her.

She tried to back up, but Drew and Laurel and Dale stood behind her, blocking her retreat. Her friends stared blankly past her, like they were hypnotized.

Then, Nicki was right in front of her. She still wore the sliver-moon earrings she was wearing the last time Mandy saw her.

"We're going to miss so much," Nicki said.

Mandy spun away. Her friends no longer blocked her path. They were gone. Everyone was gone. She sat in front of a flat panel screen that foamed with opaque mist. Two of her fingers jabbed keys frantically creating a single word, repeating it over and over:

Hahahahahahahahahahahahahahahahahahahaha hahaha ...

She woke with a start, the details of her dream instantly forgotten. Sitting up in bed, Mandy looked at the clock on the nightstand just as her mother yelled, "I'm home," from downstairs. It was a few minutes after six.

"'Kay," Mandy called.

Wiping the sleep from her eyes, Mandy walked to her computer, looked at the screen, and felt an odd sense of dread. Why her computer should scare her, she couldn't say exactly. As she sat down, she thought about something stupid Drew had said at the candlelight vigil.

She's going to miss so much.

Drew's ability to state the obvious in the most inappropriate ways was a long-standing character flaw. Everything was a romantic notion to her friend, and she didn't seem to be gifted with the filter that kept such ridiculous ideas in her head and out of her mouth. Still, for all of her clumsy speculation, Drew had actually made an interesting point.

Unlike Nicki's dream of being a veterinarian, Mandy didn't know what *she* wanted to do after school, not as a profession anyway. She presumed she would go to college and study something, figured she would get married and have kids. Over the years, she'd imagined her wedding day down to the finest detail as she sat around her room dreaming with Drew or Laurel; they'd all taken turns describing the perfect husband. These were the obvious things, events in a woman's life that she'd grown to take as givens. But they said nothing about what she wanted for herself.

Little-girl dreams of pop stardom, modeling, being a great actress had all come and gone in their time, but even when she had lip-synced into a hairbrush; or strutted in outfits before her mirror, working the runway of exposed wood by her bed; or recited lines from her favorite movies; she never really expected them to come true. They were fancies, daydreams, distractions created on boring afternoons. They made her feel giddy and silly. It was fun to pretend, but Mandy took none of those glamorous careers seriously.

So, what am I going to be, Mandy wondered. *What do I want to do?*

She knew she wanted to travel, to see the world. Her parents had taken her on family trips to New York and to Walt Disney World in Florida. They had gone hiking in the Rocky Mountains. But these trips, while fun and full of wondrous sights, were only a taste of the exploring she intended to do. All the pictures she saw in history class and poli-sci opened her eyes to a planet full of interesting places. Some places were wrapped in obvious desires: dining in Paris; shopping in Rome; skiing in Austria, shooshing down the slopes with a hottie before getting drinks in a lodge; wandering through London just because it was there. But it was the other places—places like Prague and Thailand and Istanbul, places she knew little about but that sounded exotic and different—that really excited her. There were probably a thousand such destinations, filled with amazing people waiting for her.

What am I going to miss?

It occurred to her that the greatest shame, the biggest loss would be not experiencing those unknown things. New people she would never meet, new places she would never see.

"We're going to miss so much," Nicki said.

Mandy sat down at her desk and hit the space key to shut down the screen saver. Maybe surfing the Web would help her find the right career, some profession—and not something silly like being a flight attendant—she could pursue that would open the world up to her.

But before she opened Google to start her career search, she noticed the e-mail that had been sent to her by the guy named Kyle. She had intended to erase it, until Dale showed up and started freaking out. Now, she found herself opening the note again.

Kylenevers
Subject: Me Again
Hey, sorry about yesterday. I know we don't know each other. Kyle here. I feel kind of bad about IMing you like that. With everything going on with N., I just wanted to chat . . . don't know a lot of people . . .

Mandy read the entire note twice, and though

she at first had thought it the miserable plea of a looz, she now figured he was just another kid, like her, who wanted to expand his world. She cut and pasted his screen name into the Profile Search box, just to make sure he wasn't a complete goof, like some science geek who thought dissecting rats was interesting.

Name. Kyle Nevers (Nevers: like the airport in Nantucket)
Location: Elmwood
Gender: Male . . . Born: '90s
Hobbies & Interests: How much time U got?
Favorite Gadgets: PC, cell, text: U name it, I'm there.

No picture. Not a good sign. And he certainly didn't give much away in the profile, but Mandy wasn't surprised. Most people her age knew better than to string together lists of personal information. It made it too easy for the creeps to start up a conversation. He lived in town, which struck Mandy as interesting. If he was local, he had to have attended Lake Crest High; there was no place else to go, unless . . .

Not Hammond, she thought. *Ew!* Okay, that wasn't fair. The kids at Hammond Special Studies School couldn't help being different. They had challenges, physical and mental. It's not like they were dangerous or mean or anything.

With more than a little curiosity and a bit of excitement, Mandy clicked the *Reply* button. She wrote back, telling Kyle she understood exactly what he meant about feeling weird after Nicki's death, and yes, they should chat sometime. She sent the e-mail before talking herself out of it, then leaned back in her chair.

There, she thought. *I've just met a new person. Already on my way to expanding my horizons. Kyle might become a new friend, maybe a new boyfriend (no way, stop thinking about that), and if he turns out to be creepy, I'll just block his messages. Delete him. Sending a reply was the polite thing to do. No harm in it.*

Besides, Dale would be really pissed off if he knew.

MC9010025: Do U have a pic? With everything going on, I'd feel better if I knew what U looked like.

Kylenevers: Sure. But how do U know I didn't just cut it out of a mag and scan it in? I could have downloaded it off some kid's site. It might not be me at all. LOL

MC9010025: I'll manage my own paranoia thnx. LOL

Kylenevers: Well, just 2 b sure, I've got a digital. I can take a pic now. Tell me 2 hold something like a pen or something.

MC9010025: Salute

Kylenevers: ???

MC9010025: Salute the camera like an army guy

Kylenevers: NOT!!!

MC9010025: LMAO Okay, just hold up a hairbrush or comb

Kylenevers: K brb

Mandy leaned back in her chair and waited for Kyle to send his picture. They'd been chatting ever since Mandy excused herself after dinner and ran back upstairs to see if he sent a reply to her note. Though her away message was on, Kyle had sent an IM—*just sayin hi again*—and she immediately replied.

Though their conversation was only twenty minutes old, she liked him. Kyle was funny and *not* a student at Hammond Special Studies. Since his parents moved so much on business, they'd started homeschooling him so he didn't have to endure enrolling in classes just to be yanked out before the semester ended. Things had settled down, and his family had lived in Elmwood now for nearly a whole year. Kyle assured her that was a record. *LOL*. In fact, he was technically a high school graduate, but he still studied because he wanted to get a jump on his engineering degree.

Besides, there's not much else to do.

She felt sorry for Kyle, and she envied him at the same time. Going from town to town, school to school, always having to make new friends, always leaving friends behind must have sucked, but he'd lived all over the country, seen so many places. When she asked where he used to live, he replied, *Everywhere. Ugh. LOL*.

If someone asked Mandy the same question, she'd say Elmwood. Just Elmwood. She imagined Kyle must have had wonderful stories to tell about oceans and mountains and big cities and quirky small towns. Mandy wanted to hear about every-place he'd ever been.

Kyle's photograph arrived, attached to an e-mail that read, *Happy now?* Her heart beat fast as she clicked the box to download the image. She saved it to her desktop, waited for it to finish. With her fingers trembling on the mouse, she double clicked the file and waited, holding her breath, hoping he didn't look like one of the kids at school that collected *Lord of the Rings* action fig-ures.

When the picture opened, Mandy laughed. It was a good laugh, an amused and relieved laugh. Kyle stood in a bedroom with walls painted a soft sand color. He was wearing black jeans and a white button-down shirt. His body wasn't as bulked up with muscle as Dale's, but he was tall and solid. He was blond—she'd thought he would be—and had a smooth, handsome, tanned face without a single blemish. He was very nice-looking. In fact, he was hot, even though he looked a little embarrassed in the picture. There in his left hand he held a shiny black hairbrush as she had requested. With his other hand, he saluted the camera.

MC9010025: LOL. Nice pic.

Kylenevers: Thank you, Sir.

MC9010025: LOL. Sorry bout that. Can't b 2 careful

Kylenevers: Understand. The whole thing with N creeped me so bad, I just wanted to chat with people so I didn't feel alone.

MC9010025: U don't have any friends in town?

Kylenevers: Just a buddy. We hang. Catch flicks. Play PS. It's just not the same as being part of the crowd, U know?????

MC9010025: Not really. Always been part of

the crowd

Kylenevers: U R lucky. I never got that, but maybe college

MC9010025: Definitely college. I'm sure of It

Kylenevers: Thnx. It'd b nice 2 chill in 1 place. Travel bcause I want 2 travel not bcause I have 2. Still luv 2 go places

MC9010025: Where do u want 2 go next?

Kylenevers: Brazil . . . Rio, Sao Paulo. Or maybe Prague.

MC9010025: Prague? Really? I was just thinking about it. Weird.

Kylenevers: Kewl. What were u thinking?

MC9010025: Just someplace I'd like to go.

Kylenevers: I was there once, but only a couple days. Didn't c much. 2 much running. I've spent time in most of the big European cities . . . London, Paris, Berlin, all over Italy, and I got 2 see a lot. Met kewl peeps, but not Prague. Rio would b kewl 2 though bcuz I've never been b4.

Mandy's heart beat a little faster reading his reply. He'd seen so many cool places. And she could picture Kyle there. Her imagination put him on a bustling street in London with a red double-decker bus rolling by; she saw him at the base of the Eiffel Tower, and pictured him in a gondola floating slowly along a canal in Venice. In this last daydream, she pictured herself on the bench next to him, nestled in the crook of his elbow, drifting on the water and looking out at ancient, beautiful buildings. She felt herself blush.

> **MC9010025**: Sounds amazing. I hope u get 2 go.
> **Kylenevers**: Thnx. U 2. I totally have to go somewhere soon. Definitely b4 college.
> Need some time to let the waves settle
> **MC9010025**: Waves?
> **Kylenevers**: family crap. No big deal
> **MC9010025**: We all have that
> **Kylenevers**: HEY wheres ur pic? U got mine.
> **MC9010025**: Well, u were the 1 stalking me remember. I don't have 2 prove anything. LOL
> **Kylenevers**: LOL. I'll get u 4 that.

"So, let me get this straight," Laurel said through

the phone at Mandy's ear. "The rest of us are freaking out and locked up 24/7 because Nicki died, and you're out cruising the superhighway for hottie hitchhikers?"

Mandy laughed. "It's not like that."

"You're some kind of megaho."

"I told you, *he* IM'd *me*."

"Ho."

"I am not a ho," Mandy said with another laugh. "Knock it off. God, I don't even know if I'm going to meet him or not. He's just a nice guy."

"You said he was a full-on hottie."

"He is."

"And you just want to chat with him?"

"I don't know."

"Yeah. Uh-huh. Ho."

"Whatever," Mandy said. "You're just jealous."

"Damn right," Laurel replied. "I haven't had a date in like two months, and you're lining 'em up like a boy-band producer."

"It's one guy, L."

"And Dale."

"Who is soooo yesterday."

"Said the ho."

"I'm calling Drew back. She totally understands."

"I bet," Laurel said. She changed her voice, suddenly speaking in a softer, higher tone. "Ooooooo, he sounds so dreamy. I'll bet he sneaks over to your house with roses and kisses you. He probably reads poetry and has a unit the size of your arm. Oh, tell me about him again. Oh. Tell me. Oh. Oh. Harder. Oh Kyle. Oh."

Mandy cracked up, falling over on her bed as Laurel continued to coo into the phone, imitating their friend. She laughed so hard that tears filled her eyes. "Knock it off," she said, her voice spluttering from the laughter.

"Yeah, she understands all right. Until we get her a man, she'll keep using ours and her shower massage."

"You can be such a bitch to her."

"It's all from love," Laurel said. "I love. I tease. They are my gifts."

"So, is your dad letting you come to school tomorrow?"

"Yes," Laurel said, as if the word weighed a ton. "Now that everyone knows what that guy looks like, he figures I can go places that are *populated and well lit*. His words. Not mine."

"Then you don't have to sit home all weekend,"

Mandy said, wiping the last tear from her cheek. "We can catch a movie or something."

"Definitely."

"Good. The sooner things get back to normal, the happier I'll be."

Mandy barely saw her friends over the weekend,
though they did manage to spend a couple hours
at the mall Saturday afternoon. She spent all of
Friday night online with Kyle. She liked chatting
with him, not only because he told funny stories
about all of the places she dreamed of going one
day, but also because he really seemed to understand her. Sometimes they wrote the exact same
line of text and sent them simultaneously. Then
they'd both rush to write *Jinx* and *LMAO*. They
were totally in sync with each other. Which is why
she felt bad, even a little hurt, that Kyle wasn't
online Saturday night. Mandy waited to see his
handle show up on her buddy list, but it never did.
Eventually, she turned on the television and fell

asleep. Now it was Sunday, and she planned to meet Laurel and Drew at Nicki's funeral. But Mandy was running late.

MC9010025: Everybody at skool was just weird on Fri
Kylenevers: U mentioned that.
MC9010025: Sorry. :-) It was the same way in the mall yesterday. People just wandering around, looking sad. They couldn't have all known Nicki, but it's like they did. U know?
Kylenevers: It's a tribal reaction. I've seen it a lot.
MC9010025: Tribal????
Kylenevers: Sure. It doesn't matter that they didn't know N all that well. She lived among them, part of the town, part of the tribe.

Mandy smiled. Here was another example of them being totally in sync.

MC9010025: I thought the same kind of thing the day it happened. I didn't know Nicki real well, but it felt like a really good

93

friend had died.

Kylenevers: It's natural. Every1 is looking 4 answers and scared. And they're all hurt, and they know every1 around them feels the same way. For a while it actually makes them nicer, more polite. It doesn't last.

MC9010025: Well, I wouldn't mind if the nice stuck around

Kylenevers: Believe me, compared 2 some of the places I lived, Elmwood started out plenty nice.

MC9010025: I guess. R u going to N's funeral?

Kylenevers: Can't. Brunch with family and a friend of dad's. He's a real player at Stanford U. It's 1 of the colleges high on my list, so I totally have 2 show.

MC9010025: Kewl

Kylenevers: Shouldn't you have left by now?

MC9010025: OMG! Crap. I am soooo late. Gotta go. TTFN

Kylenevers: BFN

By the time Mandy got to the chapel, it was already

full. People stood on the threshold and spilled out onto the concrete walk. Cameramen and reporters gathered near the door, and Mandy skirted them, choosing to stand on a small circle of concrete at the corner of the church. She tried to call Laurel on her cell, but for once in her life, Laurel had the phone turned off. Drew's phone was the same. So, Mandy stood on the periphery of the gathered mourners, men in black suits and women in conservative dresses and pantsuits.

She wished Kyle were there, though she totally understood him wanting to make points with the guy from Stanford. Kyle was focused on his future, and she liked that about him. Besides, Mandy had to admit, it would be pretty strange to have a first date (*okay not a date, just meeting*) at a classmate's funeral.

A man wearing a long black coat walked into Mandy's peripheral vision, and her heart skipped a beat. She turned toward him, instantly thinking of the Witchman. But it was just a mourner, making his way to the chapel doors.

When Dale pulled his Audi into the lot and parked against the curb behind a news van, she knew she wouldn't stay. At first, a spark of defiance kept her feet grounded. She wasn't going to run off just because of him. She did, however, rationalize that she couldn't see the service. She would never get in. *It'll probably go on for hours.* Besides, she had gone to the candlelight vigil. If Nicki were looking down at her, she'd totally understand.

So, Mandy slipped around the side of the church, walking up a grassy rise and back onto Summer Avenue, which would wind around to Garret Street three blocks from her house.

At home, she logged on to her computer and waited for Kyle to get home from brunch so she could tell him all about the circus at the chapel.

"So, you ditched us for a username?" Laurel said. "Not cool."

"I know. I'm sorry. We were just chatting and I wasn't watching the time. How was the service?"

"Well, I'm still a mess," Laurel said. "It was beautiful and really sweet, and I don't think I've cried that much in my life."

"How'd Drew hold up?"

"How do you think?"

"That bad?"

"Worse," Laurel said. "But hell, no one was exactly acting cool, you know?"

"I'm really sorry," Mandy said. "I should have been there."

"Damn straight. But we gotta keep livin', so I sort of forgive you. But only sort of."

"What are you doing for the rest of the afternoon?" Mandy asked.

"Talkin' to you. Talkin' to Drew. Watchin' some screen. Might actually study for that calculus test Wednesday."

"Do you think Walpern will really give us a test this week? God, nobody can even concentrate on normal things."

"You were there Friday. You heard him. He said 'test,' so I'm thinkin' test. And since calculus is the one class that wants to blow my grade point, I'm thinkin' crackin' that book might be a good idea."

"Ugh," Mandy said. "I'll never be ready by Wednesday."

"You will if you don't spend all your time chattin' with Mr. Internet Yummy Drawers."

Kylenevers: How was skool?

MC9010025: 2 words 4 ya: Calculus test.

Kylenevers: Calculus is ez.

MC9010025: So not

Kylenevers: Things back 2 normal? Sort of?

MC9010025: Again . . . so not. The teachers r. We're getting homework again, and tests!!! Ugh! But most of us r still weirded out. I can't beleev it's been a week since Nicki died.

Kylenevers: We should chat about something else.

MC9010025: I know. Ur right, but it's like being in 1 of those zombie movies

Kylenevers: You like zombie movies?

MC9010025: Not

Kylenevers: Oh.

MC9010025: I dated a guy 4 awhile and he took me 2 1. Ick!

Kylenevers: LOL. I like them even though they look so fake

MC9010025: So, uv met a lot of zombies? LOL

Kylenevers: Some. They aren't very good kissers.

MC9010025: GROSS! LMAO.

Kylenevers: Do u like 2 kiss?

MC9010025: Doesn't every1?

Kylenevers: No. Actually.

MC9010025: Well, I do.

Kylenevers: Do u think u'd like 2 kiss me?

Mandy leaned back in her chair and stared at the keyboard. This was the first time either of them had said anything remotely romantic. For all of their chatting, they usually just joked around and shared stories about their families, friends, and lives. *Did she want to kiss him?* She wanted to write *yes*, but it seemed way stupid. She didn't even know what his voice sounded like, and this realization made her feel really strange. Maybe they should talk on the phone. Or actually meet!

MC9010025: Maybe

Kylenevers: Maybe? U fraid I'm going to taste like zombie?

MC9010025: LOL! What do zombies taste like?

Kylenevers: pork chops soaked in bleach

MC9010025: Ugh! So gross.

Kylenevers: U asked.

MC9010025: Well, since I'm asking questions, do you think we could talk on the phone sometime?

Kylenevers: And ruin the magic? LOL

MC9010025: There's magic? Did I miss something ;-)

Kylenevers: LMAO. Thnx. I don't feel dissed or anything. Crap! Mom's calling me. Gotta run. Chat tomorrow?

MC9010025: Sure

Kylenevers: O! If you're serious about Prague, check out Karlstejn Castle. It's totally kewl. Way goth inside. Awesome views. It was the only thing I really got 2 C when I went.

MC9010025: K

Kylenevers: C U

MC9010025: TTFN

Kylenevers: back atcha.

Mandy smiled. She ran her cursor over the name of the castle, copied it, and then closed the IM window. She Googled the name and spent a few minutes surfing pages, looking at pictures and reading blurbs of copy about it. It really wasn't a very pretty place, she decided, but it was cool. The place looked like one of those castles they used in old, old horror movies—movies from the '60s. It was the kind of place where insane barons killed their wives in dank torture chambers, the kind of place for ghosts and vampires. One interior shot showed a massive stone room with wooden tables and a faded brown tapestry hanging from iron bars. Kyle was right; it was totally goth. Her imagination let loose, and she pictured Kyle leading her through the dark halls of Karlstejn Castle, gripping her hand tightly to guide her. They were not tourists in this place, but rather the owners—a king, a queen. Mandy shook her head, telling herself how silly she was being.

She closed the Web page.

Not quite ready to let go of Kyle for the night, she clicked on the file with his picture, and it burst across her screen. She followed the wave of his blond hair as it swept back from his forehead and looked into his clear green eyes that sparkled with embarrassment beneath the hand he used to salute her.

"Weird," Mandy said, squinting at the picture.

Somehow the image seemed different. Kyle was still a hottie holding a hairbrush and saluting her, but he seemed to have shadows on his face that she hadn't noticed before. They ran along the bottom of his cheekbones, giving him a slightly gaunt look. Something was strange about the hairbrush, also: The light that reflected on its shiny black side looked like a sharp edge rather than just a glimmer of light. Had the contrast of the picture changed somehow? That couldn't be. She'd looked at the picture a dozen times, but she hadn't done anything to manipulate the image. Maybe it was the way her desk lamp reflected off the screen that made it look wrong. It had to be something like that. Pictures didn't just change on their own.

Thursday was a day of surprises.

After school, Laurel and Drew came back to Mandy's place to hang out. Both were curious about this Kyle guy she kept talking about, so they followed her upstairs to her room and waited for her computer to boot up. When the picture opened, both of her friends pushed in close to look at the screen.

"Yeah," Laurel said, "he's got some major yummy going on."

"God, he's so cute," Drew said, already drifting into a romantic haze. "It's totally fate. I mean, if you hadn't broken up with Dale, and if Nicki hadn't been killed, you two might never have met."

"Yeah," Laurel said, "more kids should get sliced up so we can all get dates."

Drew's face fell, her dreamy voice quieting. "I just meant, it's great that something nice came out of something so bad. Jeez, Laurel."

"I'm just playin'," Laurel said, reaching out to pat Drew's knee. "It's all good."

Mandy smiled, pleased that her friends approved. She leaned back in the chair so they could get a better look and both slid a little closer to the monitor, gawking at the screen.

"I can't believe I was there when you met," Drew said.

"We haven't met."

"You know what I mean."

"Hey," Laurel said, "I thought you said he was our age."

"He is," Mandy replied. "He's seventeen."

"You sure? Boy looks like he's already got a couple of years of frat parties behind him."

"He does look older," Drew agreed. "Like my brother's age or something."

Mandy leaned forward and looked closely at the picture. The shadows on Kyle's cheeks seemed more pronounced, even more than they had the night before. Another shadow, one she hadn't noticed the night before or any other time she'd looked at the picture, lay across his brow, disappearing into the bigger shadow cast by his saluting palm. When she pulled away from the details of the pic, she had to admit Laurel and Drew were right; he did look older.

"Once," Laurel said, "I met a guy online, and he was looking all fine and boylicious. So we meet up, right? He's got this big old nasty mole on his cheek, and I'm all 'Where the hell did that come from?' I figured he Photoshopped it out of his pic or something, because this girl doesn't go for before-shots. A boy has got to complete *Extreme Makeover* before he comes callin' on the L."

"That was Hoyt, wasn't it?" Drew asked.

"Yeah, Hoyt. So, I'm all pissed off, because I'm thinkin' he was playin' me. But I get home and open his picture and there it was, right there on his face as bold as you please. I just didn't notice it before."

Mandy remembered this story now. They were freshmen at Lake Crest when it happened. Laurel spent the rest of the semester being mean to Hoyt, which seemed odd to Mandy since Hoyt didn't do anything wrong.

"Well, it's just a bad pic," Mandy said. "He shot it in like two seconds while we were chatting."

"Looks good enough to me," Laurel said.

"Yeah, and you were really smart to have him do that," Drew said. "I mean, he could have been anybody, even that scary guy that got Nicki."

The Witchman, Mandy thought, remembering his beaklike nose and pointed chin. For a few days, that image of his wild-eyed rage, was everywhere: the Internet, the news, and her own dreams.

Sometimes in the middle of the night, she woke with that old, wrinkled face hanging before her eyes, even after the nightmares he wandered into had ended.

"If we're playing show-and-tell," Laurel said, "I got something you have to see."

She got up from her seat on the bench beside Drew and walked to the bed, where she picked up her handbag. Returning to the bench, she sat down and placed the bag in her lap. From it, she pulled a small handgun out by the grip, dangling the weapon between her thumb and forefinger like it was a piece of smelly trash.

Both Drew and Mandy pulled back in shock. Drew covered her mouth with a palm, her eyes wide with astonishment.

"What are you doing with that?" Mandy asked angrily, hating the sight of the gun.

"A gift from Dad," Laurel said, still dangling the thing between her fingers. "It's not loaded yet. He won't give me the clip until I take lessons, so guess how I'm spending the next three Saturdays?"

"Why didn't you tell him you didn't want it?"

"God, I'd never have a gun," Drew said.

"Yeah, well, it was take it from him or spend the

rest of my life in my room. I figured this was the lesser of two stupids. In a few weeks, he'll chill out, and I can shove it in a box in the basement. Until then, I'm packin', girls. So, don't be dissin' me or I'll pop a cap in your asses."

"That's so not funny," Mandy said.

"Totally not," Drew agreed.

Laurel laughed and dropped the gun back in her bag. "You know I'm anti-gun. As soon as I can rid myself of it, I will."

"Your dad's really worried about you," Drew said, sounding jealous.

Mandy knew that Drew's dad was pretty much nonexistent. Including the candlelight vigil, Mandy could count the number of times she'd seen him on her fingers. He worked a lot; he'd struggled to raise Drew and her brothers on his own ever since his wife had run off to "find herself." That had been ten years ago. Apparently, Drew's mom was still lost, and so was Drew.

"My dad's a whack job. What kind of dork gives his teenage daughter a gun? I've been asking for a car for the last two years, but instead of a Beamer, I get an Uzi."

"Just keep it in your bag," Mandy said, "and don't

go telling everyone you have it."

"Right, because nothing makes you more popular than fire power. I'm not telling anyone except you guys."

The next surprise on that Thursday afternoon was for Drew. In a lot of ways, it was even more shocking than Laurel's gun show.

A ring tone had them all scrambling for their cell phones, until Drew announced, "That's mine." She looked at the caller ID before answering and turned as white as a ghost. "Oh my God!"

"What is it?" Mandy asked, thinking it had to be something terrible.

But just as she asked the question, a wide nervous smile cut across Drew's lips. "It's Jacob," she said, her voice a high squeal. "My God, Jacob Lurie is calling *me*."

"Why do I think you had something to do with this?" Mandy whispered to Laurel.

On the other side of the room, pressed into the corner, twirling her hair with a finger and clutching the cell phone to her head, Drew nodded and said, "Sure."

Laurel leaned closer and said, "I figured this was

the only way to shut her up about him. Besides, he likes her too."

"I thought you hated Jacob."

"*Hate* is such a strong word. I just feel better when I don't have to look at him. Drew's the one that's got to go out with him, not me."

Mandy nudged Laurel, knowing she was being far nicer to Drew than she'd ever admit. She'd never seen Drew so excited, though something or another often excited Drew. This was a good excited, a happy excited.

"Oh God," Drew gushed into the phone. "I know! It's totally like that."

"You realize we're going to hear about nothing else for the rest of our lives, right?" Mandy said.

Laurel's face scrunched dramatically in a pretended expression of sorrow. "I know. God help me, I know."

Mandy didn't know exactly what to make of the last two surprises of the day. After gushing and babbling about Jacob's call (*We're going to a movie tomorrow. God, I have to buy an outfit.*) Drew left in a fidgeting swirl of exhilaration. Laurel, whose father still insisted she be home before dark, left with her.

Alone, with another hour before her mom got home, and nearly two before her father would appear, Mandy signed online and immediately searched her buddy list for Kyle's handle. Disappointed that it wasn't there, she checked her e-mails. When her doorbell rang again, she was reading an announcement from Trinity King, head of the yearbook committee, informing the student body that they were dedicating a full-page memorial to Nicki Bennington. As such, they needed photographs and suggestions for text.

The doorbell rang. Mandy rose from her chair to look out the window, and was surprised to see a large green van in her driveway. A bouquet of flowers was painted on the side of the van. Beneath this, GREEN GUY FLORISTS was written in large white letters.

Flowers? she thought.

The doorbell rang again. With the thrill of anticipation urging her on, Mandy ran down the stairs, her hand hopping down the banister as she rushed for the door. She got there just as the deliveryman rang a third time.

Mandy opened the door and gasped. The man,

a roly-poly guy with thinning red hair, held a simple vase from which sprouted two dozen red roses amid a spray of baby's breath.

"Mandy Collins?" the man asked.

"Yes," she said, barely able to speak for the knot in her throat.

"You have an admirer." The man handed her the vase and made a check on his clipboard. "Have a nice afternoon."

"Thank you," Mandy said, closing the door.

She filled her eyes and nose with the wonderful flowers, holding the vase tightly so she didn't drop the gift. "Beautiful," she whispered. In the kitchen, she set the vase down on the counter and searched for a card. Kyle sent her these. She just knew it. She didn't know how he found her address—probably just looked up *Collins* in the phone book—but it didn't matter. He sent her flowers, beautiful roses. Holding the small envelope, her nervous fingers fumbled with the flap. Finally getting it open, she yanked at the card . . .

And her heart sank a little.

I'm really sorry. Dale.

Disappointed and annoyed that he would finally do something romantic after she dumped him,

Mandy carried the flowers upstairs and set them on the windowsill. Afternoon light kissed the petals and made the water-filled vase glow. *What a creep,* she thought, staring at the bouquet. What was she supposed to do now? Just ignore the gesture, move on, never mention it? Or did she have to be polite, thank him? Wouldn't that just make things harder?

"Crap," she said to the flowers. "Beautiful crap."

"Grind them up in the food processor and drop the mess on his doorstep," Laurel said over the phone. "Too little, too late. Next!"

"I'll leave those kind of dramatics to you and Drew."

"So, what are you going to do?" Laurel asked.

"I don't know. That's why I called you."

"Are you going to tell Kyle?"

"God no. This has nothing to do with him."

Mandy looked at her computer screen, more precisely at her buddy list window. Kyle still wasn't signed on. She really wanted to chat with him. He always made her feel calm and cool. Great. The one night she really needed to chat, and he pulls a vanishing act. *Where are you?*

"So, that just leaves dealing with Dale, and you've already dealt with Dale."

"So, you don't think I should call and thank him? I mean, it's a pretty big deal if you think about it."

"Big deal? His daddy's got more scratch than Puffy. He could send you a car, and it wouldn't be a big deal to him. As far as I'm concerned, he's still got some lesson to learn."

"Okay, L," Mandy said. "Jeez, I thought you liked Dale."

"Dale is fine, as in fine face, fine bod, and *fin*ancially secure, but he treated you wrong. You did the right thing. You gotta look out for yourself."

Later in the evening, near eleven, Mandy shut down her computer. The last surprise of the day was that Kyle never signed on. He never even wrote her an e-mail. She went to bed worried she'd done or said something to make him mad. That was silly, of course. She didn't do anything. The last time they chatted, he was in a good mood, only signing off because his mom needed him for something.

But you mentioned talking on the phone, Mandy thought. He made a couple of jokes, then suddenly had to go. Was there a reason he didn't want to talk to her, something about his voice? Maybe he sounded like Mickey Mouse. She didn't know, but the question ran through her mind and, like a lullaby, carried her off to sleep.

Friday was just awful for Mandy. She woke up expecting to find an e-mail from Kyle, but her inbox only harbored spam and five notes from Drew, all about the date she was having with Jacob. After the third e-mail—*OMG. I STILL can't believe this!*—Mandy signed off and got ready for school.

After nine days, most things at Lake Crest, while not back to normal, were at least tolerable. Classes returned to being informational, if not interesting, and her friends were in high spirits, Drew especially. Still, for Mandy it was horrible. She spent the whole day ducking her head when she saw Dale, scurrying down hallways that took her to places she didn't need to be, and once even hiding in the girls' restroom when she spotted him down the hall.

Fortunately, they didn't share any classes. It didn't make the day easy, just easier. Nothing was going to make the day easy.

During her free period, Mandy went outside for some air. The crush of students in the halls, the fear of seeing Dale again, was just too much to handle. The sun shone brightly, though the day was chill. She hugged herself and walked around the main building, past the niche in the wall where the smokers gathered, toward the "Patio."

The Patio was a broad slab of white concrete. There were about a dozen tables surrounded by metal chairs. During good weather a lot of kids ate their lunch there, but it was getting cooler and the area was pretty much abandoned until spring came. That's why Mandy was surprised to see a handful of students gathered at a single table. Fiona Charlotte, a senior girl who was usually ignored, paced beside the table. She was moving her hands frantically while the other kids watched her.

". . . totally like Jack the Ripper," Mandy heard Fiona say as she approached.

"You mean he took her ovaries and junk?" Tim Wayland asked.

"No," Fiona said excitedly, all but dancing on the concrete. "He didn't take anything. He's not a collector, that's what my dad calls them. But he like . . . played with stuff. Moved stuff, you know?"

"Jack the Ripper took their ovaries and junk," Tim said, as if he hadn't made his point clear the first time.

"Whatever!" Fiona replied. "I'm just saying Nicki was totally messed up . . . inside. Okay? It was like he cut her open and did all of this gross stuff. She was totally butchered."

Mandy's stomach clenched, disgusted by Fiona's performance. A thick lump lodged in her throat, and she held herself tighter.

"Like what?" Ian Page asked. He sounded eager, like Fiona was describing a sexual event. The knot in Mandy's stomach rolled.

How could they do this? How could they talk about Nicki like she was some distant celebrity whose tragedy was nothing more than entertainment?

"He squeezed some of the organs," Fiona said. "Like squeezed them till they popped. My dad said it was a total mess in there. Just soup."

"Ohhhhh nasty," Ian said with a laugh. "Nicki stew."

The other kids laughed nervously, some lowered their heads and shook them back and forth. "Totally!" Fiona exclaimed. "My dad's been on the police force for like a million years, and he said he's never seen anything this full-on gross."

Mandy backed away from the table and her excited classmates. They were awful. God, they were just so awful. She turned and ran back to the front of school, tears brimming in her eyes.

After school, Mandy and her friends went to Bodyworks. She wanted to get Fiona Charlotte's cruel and amused voice out of her head. *Cut. Butchered. Totally Jack the Ripper.* She didn't say a word to Laurel or Drew, because she just wanted to forget, though she doubted she ever would.

She was totally butchered.

They changed into their workout clothes and met at the elliptical machines. Once they programmed their routines, Drew dove into exercise and pumped her legs like her life depended on it.

"Do you think I could lose like ten pounds if I

just kept running until my date with Jacob?"

"Cutting off your head would do it," Laurel said.

Mandy winced at the comment.

"I just wish I had more time to get ready," Drew said, panting now. "I so wasn't expecting him to call."

"Well, your ass wasn't too fat for him to call in the first place, so it probably isn't too fat now," Laurel said.

"What if he hates me?" Drew asked.

"He won't hate you," Mandy said, rolling her eyes.

"No more than anybody else," Laurel added.

"You're so mean," Drew said, a drop of sweat rolling down her cheek. "I mean, I'm about to have a total nervous breakdown, and you're all bitchy. It's only like the most important thing to me ever."

"It's just a date," Laurel said. "Quit hemorrhaging. He likes you. And hell, at least you get to go out. I have to stay home with Dad and clean my gun."

Mandy and Drew just shook their heads.

After twenty minutes, Mandy was exhausted and Drew looked like she'd just stepped out of a shower. Laurel announced it was time for abs, and

Mandy groaned. She was so tired. Last night was rough. Asleep, she'd had terrible dreams. Awake, she'd worried what to do about Dale and Kyle. And the fear was back. The fear she'd felt in the days following Nicki's death had returned, thanks to Fiona.

He said he's never seen anything this full-on gross.

"You guys have to meet," Laurel said, startling Mandy. "Unless you just don't want to, and then you have to delete him, because you can't chat forever."

"I know."

"Has Kyle asked you to meet?" Drew asked, finishing her crunches and dropping back to the mat.

"No," Mandy said. "Do you think that's weird?"

"Right now, everything is weird, and I'm lookin' out for my girls. Don't want you gettin' in too deep with Mr. I-don't-think-so. If he doesn't want to meet, then he's got glitches. Best to find out early so you aren't all *English Patient* with him."

"She's right," Drew said. "You should make sure."

"Oh, *now* listen to her," Laurel said, her voice high and amused. "She's going on her first date in like two years, and she's all knowledgeable."

"God, Laurel, I'm just agreeing with you. Check your meds."

"Yeah," Mandy said. "You're right. Next time we chat, I'll ask."

"Good," Laurel said, springing to her feet. "Let's go work lats."

After the workout, with no time for the juice bar that afternoon, the three girls gathered in the parking lot. Laurel continued to make jokes at Drew's expense, and Mandy found herself tiring of the banter. All she wanted to do was go home, log on, and have a quiet night chatting with Kyle. (*If he's even online tonight.*) But Drew's anxiety over her impending date and Laurel's overpossessive father worked together to cancel Mandy's plan.

"You have to help me get ready," Drew said. "What if I go out and meet Jacob and I've got like a huge stain on the butt of my dress or something?"

"Help her out," Laurel said. "I'd do it, but if I'm not home in twenty minutes, Dad is going to blow a vein."

"All right," Mandy said. Her lackluster response brought a frown from Drew.

This is a huge deal to her, Mandy thought, feeling bad. *If Kyle is online, he'll still be there when I get home.*

Mandy put on a big smile and arched her eyebrows. "Quit moping," she told Drew. "This is the biggest night of your life, and we've got to make you fabulous. Frown lines are not fabulous, so knock it off."

Seeing that Mandy was finally taking her date with Jacob seriously, Drew smiled wide and switched into hyperdrive. "I've got to shower again, do my hair, and you have to pick an outfit for me because, God, I hate everything I have."

Drew had already set off across the parking lot, speaking more to herself than to either Laurel or Mandy. Her hands danced around her head as she emphasized all of the things she needed to do before meeting Jacob.

"Once you get our girl set up, why don't you come chill at my place?" Laurel asked. "We can watch some screen, eat some pizza."

"You're not going to let me say no, are you?" Mandy asked.

"Oh, so now it's like some huge favor to hang out with the glamorous L?"

"It's not that. I wanted to chat with Kyle tonight, you know?"

"I have a computer," Laurel reminded. "In fact, I have *the* computer. Makes yours look like a dusty old adding machine. Besides, I might have a few words of my own for that man of yours."

After a shower, Mandy helped get Drew's hair to lie right, and then slapped at her hands every time Drew reached up to fiddle with it. She gave make-up tips, having Drew ease up on the eye shadow but insisting she give her lashes another pass with the mascara brush. Then, they rummaged through Drew's closet for the right clothes. Drew wanted to wear a nasty green dress that made her look like a cheap hooker. Instead, Mandy put together an outfit with a black blouse and snug khaki slacks that made her look amazing.

"And wear a low heel. You don't know if you're going to be doing a lot of walking or not."

"You're the best."

"Was there a particular reason you were trying to cultivate the ho look?"

Drew turned away from the mirror, feigning shock. She laughed and slapped at Mandy's shoulder.

"I wasn't going to look like a whore. I just want him to like the way I look."

"He already likes the way you look. That's why he asked you out."

"I'm just so nervous."

Mandy shook her head and stepped forward to give her friend a hug. Mandy knew that Drew felt things more intensely than she or Laurel did. It was usually annoying, but this evening, she felt like a big sister sending her kid sister out for the first time.

"I'm such a dork," Drew said into Mandy's shoulder. "I'm a stupid dork and Jacob is going to hate me."

"He's not going to hate you, Drew. Not unless he's a total looz."

"Really?"

"Really," Mandy said.

Drew returned to the mirror to look at herself, pulling at the hem of her blouse and smoothing the fabric of her slacks with long strokes along the thighs.

Mandy's cell phone buzzed, and she looked away, pulling the unit from her jacket. Another text message. Like the message she received at Nicki's vigil, no username appeared with the note, and though the message might have been harmless enough, it unnerved her to see it without attribution.

CULOR

Of course, the message came from Laurel. Mandy wasn't expecting to see anyone else that night. Still, she looked at the screen, and it made her uncomfortable. She rationalized, telling herself it was likely a glitch in her cell phone service. Maybe her screen was broken or some signal had whacked the display. None of these explanations removed the electric tingle of fear from her skin.

"Who is it?" Drew asked, reaching a palm toward her perfectly fixed hair.

"Don't touch the 'do," Mandy warned, closing her phone. "It was just Laurel," she said, feeling almost certain that it wasn't.

"Probably something nasty about me."

"No," Mandy said. "It didn't have anything to do with you."

Mandy had hoped that Jacob would give her a lift to Laurel's before sweeping Drew off on their date. Though early in the evening, it was already dark, and she didn't want to walk alone. Drew's father wasn't home, and her brothers had already gone out for the evening, so she had her digits crossed for Jacob. But when he arrived, she saw it wasn't going to happen. Jacob had borrowed his dad's convertible, a sweet little black BMW roadster. No back seat. Only room for two. She supposed Drew could sit on her lap, but that was a less-than-glamorous way to kick off a first date.

The three of them chatted briefly, and again, feeling like an older sister, Mandy hugged Drew and sent her off. Her friend grinned nervously in the passenger seat when Jacob gunned the engine and sped away.

Alone on the walk in front of Drew's house, Mandy hugged herself and looked around the neighborhood. Lights burned behind all of the windows. People wandered through living rooms and dining rooms. For most, it was suppertime. Not late at all.

CUL8R

Mandy stepped off the walk, crossed the street, and headed to Laurel's. A sense of being watched lay over her like a shawl, but she knew it was just lingering paranoia. The Witchman was long gone, probably in Mexico by now, or lying low in some shack three states over. Still, Mandy walked a little faster, checking every yard and sidewalk. She didn't really think about the direction she was going.

It wasn't until she approached the library property that Mandy even remembered it was on her way. But the moment she saw the trees rise up, separating Drew's housing development from the one where she and Laurel lived, Mandy's pulse began to race.

That's where the Witchman took Nicki. Those trees were the last nice things Nicki ever saw.

She was totally butchered.

Mandy crossed the road to put distance between herself and the library. Though the far side of the street was lined with shrubs and an other stand of trees, she didn't care. She was more worried about being too close to the place where Nicki died.

Walking quickly, head down, ears peeled for any sounds, she pulled her cell phone from her jacket. She'd call Laurel. A familiar voice would help. That way, Mandy wouldn't feel so alone.

She dialed, put the phone to her ear, and looked up to see that she was alone on the walk. Across the street, she saw the library. The sight of it chilled her. A cone of light from the floods under its eaves spilled over the edge of the parking lot into the tall brown weeds at the side of the building. This was the same view she'd seen on the news.

Come on, Laurel, pick up.

The phone rang twice and a hiss of static filled her ear. "Laurel?" she asked. The static rippled like someone crumpling a paper bag, pausing, then crumpling again. "Laurel. It's me, Mandy. Laurel?"

"This isn't Laurel," a rasping voice said. Whoever was on the line sounded old.

He also sounded amused. Behind his voice, that crunching, crumpling sound grew faint and then burst forward, nearly deafening her.

"I'm sorry," she said into the phone. Her speed dial must have glitched, and she got the wrong number. "Good-bye."

"See you later," the man said. The word was followed by what sounded like a cough. Or a laugh. Then the static erupted and the line went dead.

CUL8R

Mandy looked at the phone, terrified. Her heart thumped hard in her chest. Behind her, in the brush that ran beside the sidewalk, a twig snapped. Branches rustled.

She ran. At first she sprinted down the side-walk, but her fear intensified. Someone could leap out of the bushes, drag her in. *Oh God*. Checking for traffic ahead and behind her, Mandy ran into the middle of the road. In her mind, terrible things happened: the Witchman shot out of the brush, his stooped form moving with inhuman speed to catch her, he appeared as if by magic in the road ahead of her, one long finger pointing at her chest before he raced forward and lifted her from the street; he threw her over his shoulder, carrying her screaming to his special place behind the library, where he would . . .

Cut her open. . . . She was totally butchered.

Mandy let out a cry of fear and ran faster, trying to keep the Witchman out of her head. But it didn't work. With every step, his beaklike nose, his pointed chin, his wild eyes were with her. The fear of his outstretched fingers reaching for her back made her charge desperately down the street.

The familiar houses of her development, aglow with lights, fell in around her. She slowed her pace, caught her breath. A couple, chatting quietly, walked their dog on the sidewalk ahead. Behind the walls and windows of the homes, men, women, boys, and girls sat down to dinner. TVs showed syndicated reruns of popular sitcoms and the national evening news. Eight blocks away, her mother would just be getting home from work.

It was still early, but for Mandy it felt very late.

Laurel held the slice of double cheese pizza in front of her mouth and looked at Mandy like she'd just said, "I want to work the drive-through window at Meaties." Laurel put down the slice and wiped at her lips with a finger as if she'd actually taken a bite. "You're trippin'," Laurel said. "I didn't text-mess you."

They sat in the kitchen of Laurel's house with a large pizza that had arrived two minutes after Mandy. Mandy didn't want any. She was still scared, and the fear tied a knot in her stomach, twisted it up tight so she couldn't even think about eating. She could barely get sips of iced tea through the tension in her throat. She was so upset, and all she wanted was some kind of rational explanation. The message must have come from Laurel.

"That's not funny, L."

"And I'm not joking, M."

"I called here."

"But the phone didn't ring. Look, when have I ever been down with practical jokes? That was Naughty Nic's bag, not mine. Yeah, I get my giggle on bustin' some chops, but I don't play the mind screw."

"Then who sent that message?"

"Uh, Dale?"

"No," Mandy said. "The more I think about it, the more I'm sure he didn't do it. Hiding his ID like that would be too complicated for him. Even asking Matthew to do it would be too much effort."

"What about your new boy, Kyle?"

"I didn't even know Kyle the night of Nicki's vigil."

"Doesn't mean he didn't know you."

"Oh, come on," Mandy said. "That's ridiculous. Why would he?"

Laurel shrugged and retrieved her pizza from the plate. She took a bite and pulled back, cheese stretching like suspension wires between her mouth and the slice. She washed the bite down with a swig of her iced tea and leaned back in the chair.

"Your problem is, you're too rational," Laurel

said. "You expect everyone else to act rationally. But that's not how people are. They want to be, and they can explain every weird-ass thing they do, but that doesn't make them rational. Even psychos got reasons. It's that method-to-the-madness thing. Now, you think someone is playing you, and you figure it's got to be someone that has a reason to be playin'. I'm just sayin' that some folks don't need a reason. Some folks get *their* giggle on just knowin' you're scared, whether they know *you* or not."

Mandy tried to think of an argument, but everything she considered struck her as overly rational. Laurel was making sense.

"And let's not forget," Laurel continued, "people say 'see you later' all the time. Now, I can see why you got the creeps in you. I won't go anywhere near that library myself these days, but it's not exactly a death threat, you know?"

"It was that voice, though," Mandy said. "When I thought I was calling you. The guy's voice."

"Old people are scary," Laurel said.

Mandy laughed.

"It's not that he was old. He just sounded, I don't know . . . He sounded wrong, but I can't really describe it. It seems kind of stupid now. Maybe it was just being by the library that scared me."

"Let's talk about it upstairs," Laurel said. "Dad is floating around in the living room, and I don't need him finding something new to freak over. He'd probably make me drive a tank to school or something."

"Okay."

"Now, eat. Or I'll put this fine cheesiness away by myself, and my skin so doesn't need that."

Before going up to Laurel's room, Mandy picked at a single slice of pizza. Her appetite didn't return, and the whole thing seemed to be annoying the hell out of Laurel. In her room, with Mandy sitting on the bed, Laurel went to her computer and killed the screen saver. Her wallpaper, a field of bright yellow sunflowers, burst across the monitor.

"The first thing to do," Laurel said, "is forget about that phone call. We both know that nobody can jack into a line like that, unless they're FBI or magic or something. The signal got mixed up, and you called a wrong number. Unfortunately, you got some old dude with Satan's voice who says 'see you later' instead of 'bye.'"

"I know," Mandy said. But part of her didn't know. At the time, she'd immediately connected the wrong-sounding old man with the earlier message. It was hard to sever that connection now, no matter what Laurel said.

"So, that really only leaves the text messages." Laurel typed while she spoke. "And, I think I have an answer to that. When we were talking downstairs, I remembered something. Here, come read."

Mandy walked across the room and leaned over Laurel's shoulder to look at the screen. Her friend had loaded a news page from a tech site with the headline Cell Phones New Frontier for Hackers. She read the first two paragraphs, which described a series of cell-phone specific viruses.

"Does it say anything about receiving blind messages like I have?"

"No," Laurel said. "But they only talk about a few of the service problems people have with these. See, a hacker doesn't know anything about you, but he's groovin' on knowing that he's messin' with your life and everybody else's. It's like I was sayin'."

Mandy read another paragraph of the article, but

every third word was tech slang that she didn't understand, so she gave up. She'd take Laurel's word for it. After all, it made perfect sense. Neither of the messages, when taken out of context, was threatening in the least. One was just *hahaha*, and the other *CUL8R*, one of the most common phrases she'd come across. She used it herself.

"God," Mandy said. "What jerks."

"True enough," Laurel agreed. "But before you call customer service, let's check out one more thing."

"Okay. What?"

"Kyle."

MC9010025: Missed u lst night
Kylenevers: Sorry. Parents dragged me out. :—(What's up?
MC9010025: At a friend's 2night. Saw u online.
Kylenevers: It's my life LOL
MC9010025: LOL. Can't chat long. She'll be back in a minute.

Mandy turned to Laurel with a smile and winked. Laurel nudged her with a shoulder.

Kylenevers: b home l8r?

MC9010025: Probably stay here

Kylenevers: Oh. Drag. Hoping we could chat.

"Ask him," Laurel said.

"Check your meds. I'm going to."

MC9010025: Me too. Hey! Friends and I are getting together at Corey's that restaurant by the mall tomorrow. U should come.

Mandy felt Laurel's arm snake around her neck as her friend leaned in close to read Kyle's reply. Mandy waited anxiously, but it was taking Kyle a long time to answer.

"He's going to bail," Laurel said. "Boy has got glitches."

"Just wait. Let's see what he says."

Kylenevers: Ugh. Can't . . .

"What did I say?" Laurel asked, tapping Mandy's shoulder.

Kylenevers: Remember my brunch last Sun?

MC9010025: Sure

Kylenevers: Got an early acceptance to Stanford. Have a campus tour on Wed and a meeting with counselor on Thurs. My parents are making a vacation out of it. Ugh. LOL. I just found out we're leaving Mon morning, so my weekend is kind of screwed. What about next weekend? By then, I'll need to recharge. Sat night?

MC9010025: k. Sounds good.

Kylenevers: Awesome. It's a date.

MC9010025: Kewl. Chat l8r. Friend coming back. TTFN

Kylenevers: BFN

"Doesn't mean anything," Laurel said defensively. "He's got all week to bail on you."

Oddly enough, Mandy was thinking the exact same thing.

The next morning, Mandy sat at a gleaming white table across from Drew. Most of the dread of the previous evening had faded, and Mandy felt a sense of calm sitting with her friend. They were in Corey's, the restaurant Mandy mentioned to Kyle the night before. Corey's was a modern diner with a floor tiled in black marble and high-tech light fixtures that looked like little Chinese hats. The place reminded Mandy of her own house, all slick and polished. As a result, she didn't usually like Corey's much, but this was where her friends gathered to drink coffee, gossip, and as was now the case, download information.

"We had the best time," Drew said, sounding like it was the most unexpected thing to ever happen. "He's just so cool, and did you see his car?"

Mandy was going to remind Drew that the BMW belonged to Jacob's father, but decided to let her friend enjoy the fantasy. "Yes. How cool was that?"

"I know. My God. Everyone was looking at us. I couldn't believe it. It was like a fairy tale."

As Drew spilled out the details of her date—the restaurant where they had dinner, the movie they saw, the coffee place they went to afterward—she emphasized the story with broad hand gestures and enough *God*s to fill a sermon. Mandy looked at her friend with a smile. Nodded her head. And though she was trying to listen, keeping her ears alert for key words and pauses that required a response, her mind wandered. She remembered her dates with Dale: how he'd taken her to homecoming, even though he was sick with the flu; how they took turns picking films to watch, whether on DVD or at the movies; the way he held her just tightly enough when they kissed. She wondered if she would have these kinds of memories with Kyle, and she suddenly thought she would not. He was lines of text on a computer screen. He wasn't real yet, might never be real.

It occurred to Mandy then that Kyle might simply be a rebound. He was funny and seemed nice, and he was certainly good-looking, but if she was spending so much time thinking about Dale and their wonderful times together, she had to believe that she missed him. And how could she miss someone she didn't want or like?

Mandy made herself stop thinking about that. It was silly. Sure, she had a good time with Dale, but that didn't mean he was right for her. A lot of good traits didn't mean there weren't bad ones. She was just confused about Kyle. Last night, Laurel made a big deal about him having glitches. She spent most of the night talking about it. Sure, a lot of it was joking, but her concerns and warnings sank in. Besides, hearing all of the romantic details of Drew's date was bound to kick up fond memories.

"And when he kissed me good night," Drew said, "I could barely stay on my feet. I almost fainted. I swear."

"That sounds amazing," Mandy told her. "When's he supposed to call again?"

"He already did," Drew said, her cheeks bursting with blush. "This morning, just before I left. We're going to meet at the mall later and look at CD players. Jacob needs a new system for his room."

Mandy was about to offer another exclamation of joy for her friend, but the door to the restaurant opened and a familiar face appeared in the lobby. "Crap," she said.

Dale stood in front of the hostess stand, looking around the restaurant as if searching for friends. When he spotted Mandy, he went rigid and looked at the floor.

"What?" Drew asked. "You don't think I should go?"

Drew was so caught up in her new romance that she was oblivious to everything else. Mandy looked into her coffee cup, hoping her hair would cover most of her face.

"Dale's here," she whispered.

"Let's leave," Drew said, all but panicked.

"Check your meds," Mandy told her. She straightened up, feeling silly for having tried to hide. "I'm not going to let him run my life."

Upon finishing this defiant statement, she glanced back at the lobby. Dale was halfway to their table, looking right at her. Maybe bailing wasn't such a bad idea.

"Hey, Drew," he said when he reached the table.

"Hi, Dale."

"Mandy."

"Dale."

She clutched her coffee mug between her hands, trying to keep them from shaking. Butterflies went full-on hyperdrive in her stomach. She searched for her cool, but couldn't find it. Having him standing so close just freaked her. And it didn't help that he was wearing the sky-colored sweater Mandy gave him for Christmas.

"How're you doing?" Dale asked.

"Fine," Mandy said.

"Do you think we could talk?" he asked.

"I have to go!" Drew announced too loudly, already retrieving her bag and standing from the booth. "I have to meet Jacob. He's buying a new stereo for his room, and he really wants me to help him pick it out. You know how guys are. So ... okay ... bye."

Amazed, Mandy stared at her escaping friend. *How could you?* Mandy wanted to ask. Drew looked back at her with an expression of wide-eyed desperation. Not knowing how to handle the situation, Drew chose to get away from it, as fast as her little traitorous legs would take her.

"She's dating Lurie?" Dale asked, taking the recently vacated space in the booth. "That makes sense."

"What's that supposed to mean?" Mandy asked.

"Nothing," Dale said, lifting Drew's abandoned coffee and sipping from the mug. "Jacob's cool. Drew is cool. It makes sense."

That's not what he meant, Mandy thought. He was probably going to say something nasty, but knew it would piss her off even more than she already was, which would be quite an accomplishment, considering how she felt.

"Let's talk," Dale said, putting down the mug. "How're you doing?"

Mandy refused to reply. At least, that's what she told herself when she could think of nothing to say.

"Did you get the flowers?"

"Yes."

"Lame, right?" he said with a nervous laugh.

"They were beautiful," she said through a tight jaw. "Thank you."

"You're welcome," he said. Dale tapped on the table with his index finger and looked at the room over Mandy's shoulders. "So, here's the thing. The guys and I were talking, right? And they've been calling me an ass since all of this happened."

"They have?" Mandy was shocked.

"Sure. They're not the cavemen you think they are. Anyway, they laid into me about being lousy to you, said I should have shown a lot more respect. And it's like, I didn't get it. I *so* didn't get it." Dale let out a chirp of a laugh, continued to tap on the table. "So, my dad and I were watching the game the other night, and I told him what was going on, right? I told him I screwed up with you because I was messing around online. I told him about me coming to your house and acting stupid. You know what he said?"

"No. What did he say?"

"He said that I was young and shouldn't worry about one girl. The world was full of girls, and I could have as many of them as I wanted. He pointed at the game, right? His finger's all jabbing at those basketball players on the television, and he's saying, 'You think any of those guys worries about what one girl thinks? Even their wives? Hell no.'"

"Charming," Mandy said, picking up her mug and taking a sip.

"Yeah," Dale whispered. "That's the thing, right? I see how miserable he is, and how miserable Mom is, and I never got it before. I mean, most people think we've got it all, right? But neither one of them is happy, and I suddenly got it. That's why I sent you those flowers."

"I don't understand," Mandy said.

"They have everything, and they don't really appreciate anything. Right? I mean, I don't know why. I don't know what else they want, but they must want something or they'd be happy. And it freaked me out because I've got this middle-aged *really* unhappy guy telling me I was doing the right thing. That's when I knew that I really, really screwed up."

The butterflies in her stomach quieted. Her mind, which had been on red alert, ready to shoot back clever and biting retorts to his excuses, calmed. She had expected little from Dale, nothing more than what he'd said at her house before she slammed the door on him, but what he was saying now surprised her. She didn't know what to say.

"So look, here's the deal," Dale continued. "I'm probably going to keep being a big dumb guy for a while. But I'm trying to be a little less dumb. I don't expect you to take me back, okay? But I want to apologize again. No excuses. I screwed up. It was stupid messing around online. And I'm sorry."

"He did not," Laurel said.

"Yes, he did. I got that feeling like I was about to start crying, and I think if he'd said anything else, I would have."

"You think he was playin'?"

"No," Mandy said. "He was not playin'." She adjusted the cell phone against her head while she poured a glass of iced tea, and then leaned back against the kitchen counter. "Totally *not* playing."

"So what's Girl going to do now?"

"I don't know," Mandy said. "I mean, we're not back together or anything. It's just so weird."

"There's hope for boykind yet. So, ask me about gun practice."

"How was gun practice?"

"Girl, don't ask," Laurel said, then broke up laughing. "I sat in a room with a bunch of losers for four hours listening to some redneck extol the magical wonder of poppin' a cap. We didn't even get a shot off. That's for next week. So, I still have this thing and no bullets. Dad is upset. He thinks I should have a license to kill by now."

"I hate those things."

"Yes, you and Princess Drew have made that clear enough."

"After what she did, running out on me, you ought to pop a cap in her."

"Yeah, except it worked out good, so I can save a bullet."

"I guess so."

Mandy lay on her bed staring at the ceiling. For the first time in weeks she didn't feel like something terrible was about to happen. In fact, she felt good. Finally, the dark cloud that hung over her since the night she'd caught Dale flirting online and since Nicki died was dissipating. She thought about what Dale said to her, thought again how great he looked in the sweater she'd given him. What she didn't know, though it teased her, was whether the conversation with him gave her closure on their relationship or opened the door for them to try again. It was hard not to think about it.

And naturally, when she thought about Dale, she thought about Kyle. How could she not? They were supposed to go out on Saturday night, but

Mandy felt none of the excitement she usually did when a boy asked her out. Maybe it was being asked via IM, or the fact that Laurel was with her when Kyle asked. Mandy couldn't be certain, but if Kyle was nothing more than a rebound, she'd know now. It would have to be totally obvious. If he wasn't, and she really liked him, that would be obvious too. Wouldn't it?

Laurel thought so. She told Mandy that her head should be clear now, and with that clarity came the possibility of choosing between Dale and Kyle. ("Are these my only choices?" she had joked.) Again, she told herself that Kyle wasn't really real. He was just lines of type in an instant message window. But that wasn't fair. In fact, it was kind of selfish and bitchy. Behind those lines was a person, a young man with feelings.

Do u think u'd like 2 kiss me?

Kyle had asked her that, and she'd said maybe. If he were standing in her room right then and asked, she'd say yes. Absolutely. Please. Because she needed to know what she felt about him. Was he just a distraction, something to kill time so she didn't have to spend every minute thinking about Dale or Nicki? Could she really use someone that way, even if it was totally subconscious? She hoped not.

But there was a lingering doubt, and more and more, she believed she could.

"Ugh," she said to the ceiling. She was starting to bring that dark cloud back. She had to think about something else. She decided to think about the trips she'd like to take once school was out.

Where should I go? she wondered. *There are so many places to see. How do you pick just one?*

MC9010025: If u could go on vacation anywhere, where would u go?
Kylenevers: ????
MC9010025: I was thinking about it this afternoon. U mentioned Brazil.
Kylenevers: Did I? U going someplace?
MC9010025: Worried?
Kylenevers: Maybe. :-) When r u going?
MC9010025: After graduation. It would b fun 4 Laurel and Drew and I 2 travel a little b4 college.
Kylenevers: OK. Sure. What about Prague? I thought that was high on your list.
MC9010025: Brazil sounds more exotic.

Kylenevers: U don't want 2 go 2 Brazil.
Not unless u know people. It's kind of
weird down there.
MC9010025: Do u know people there?
Kylenevers: Some
MC9010025: So introduce me LOL
Kylenevers: Nah. I'm keeping u 4 myself.
LOL
MC9010025: LOL. U think I'm urs huh?
Kylenevers: U tell me

Mandy didn't know. There was something
romantic about not meeting, like they had the
chance to really get to know each other before all
of the physical stuff started. In English class, Mr.
Stahlman talked about two poets who wrote to
each other for a long time and by the time they
actually met, they were already in love. They didn't
even know what the other looked like, and based
solely on letters, lines of text like the ones she read
from Kyle, they fell in love. The poets' names were
Elizabeth Barrett and Robert Browning, and their
relationship was beautiful and historic. But Mandy
had a hard time even thinking about her chats
with Kyle as a relationship. Sitting in her desk

chair, staring at the screen, she thought it all felt kind of hollow. How could anyone know if the person writing was telling the truth? You had to see someone's face when they shared their lives with you. Maybe modern people were just more cynical. Maybe it was just Kyle.

MC9010025: Maybe
Kylenevers: Ugh. Another maybe. First the kiss. Now this. U R going 2 b tough, I can tell.
MC9010025: LOL. So, when do u actually leave for Stanford?
Kylenevers: Mon morning. Tomorrow family stuff and packing. Back Fri.
MC9010025. Will u b online?
Kylenevers: I'm always online. LOL

Tuesday afternoon in the cafeteria, while Kyle was somewhere in California adding another city to the long list of those he'd visited, Mandy listened while Drew raved about her new boyfriend. Everything was "Jacob said," and "Jacob did," and "Jacob thinks." Laurel was there too, occasionally making faces at Mandy, often shaking her head in wonder. But, for Drew's benefit, both kept their smiles stretched wide. Neither of them had seen their friend this happy, ever.

"He's already talking about the prom," Drew said, her cheeks blossoming with blush for the twentieth time since lunch period started. "The prom! God, do you know what that means?"

"I think it's a big dance at the end of the school year," Laurel said.

"Ha, ha," said Drew, shaking her head in annoyance.

Mandy was suddenly struck with a very odd and kind of funny image. She pictured herself at the prom, amid glittering decorations and flashing lights, dancing with her computer screen. Lines of text rolled over it while a slow number gave a rhythm for her feet. She paused and introduced the computer to her friends. *This is my date, Kyle. Kyle this is . . .*

"Dale," Laurel whispered.

"What?" Mandy asked, already scoping the cafeteria for him. "Where?"

"At the cola vend."

Mandy looked across the room over the heads of dozens of kids eating their lunches and found the row of vending machines and Dale sliding a dollar into the one on the far left. Seeing him, even so far away, sent tingles through her body.

"Has he called?" Drew asked.

"No," Mandy said. "Why would he call?"

"I don't know. You said he apologized and stuff. I thought he might've called."

Drew was a terrible liar. Fear of getting caught always covered her face like a stain when she tried. She was lying now.

"Drew," Mandy said, her voice low with warning. "What do you know?"

"I don't know anything," Drew replied, looking down at her lunch. She made to grab for a carrot stick, then tried for a cube of white cheese. Finally, she grabbed her diet soda and shrugged. "Don't know what you're talking about."

"Did you talk to Dale?" Mandy asked, a tremor of excitement running through her.

"I promised not to say anything," Drew said into the mouth of her soda.

"Promises to the opposite sex don't count," Laurel said. "It's like making a promise to your dog. Really. That's the first rule of dating. Now, spill."

"He called last night," Drew said, looking sheepishly at Mandy. "He wanted to know if you said anything about Saturday."

Mandy was suddenly filled with dread, remembering how she'd downloaded everything she felt to Drew that night on the phone. "What did you say?" Mandy asked, now furious with her friend.

"Nothing," Drew said, cowering behind her soda can.

"Oh? Let's move on to the torture phase," Laurel said. In a flash she yanked her cell phone from the pocket of her slacks. "I have a certain Jacob Lurie's digits. What do you imagine Mandy and I could tell him?"

Wide-eyed, Drew gasped. "You can't."

"I see no fundamental difference in each situation," Laurel replied, rocking the cell phone in her hand casually. "Now, let's start at the beginning. We'll decide your punishment later."

Drew spilled. Her voice trembled and cracked as she told them Dale asked if Mandy said anything about getting back together, and "I totally told him you didn't." He'd asked if Mandy still thought he was a jerk, and "I said, you really appreciated his apology and thought it was a cool thing for him to do." And he asked if Drew thought he should try calling or if that would just piss Mandy off, and "I told him he should call."

"And?" Mandy asked.

"That's it," Drew said. "I swear. He just told me how bad he's felt since that night and what a screw-up he is and that he didn't deserve you and stuff."

"He said that?"

"God, yes. Like fifty billion times."

"What else?" Laurel asked, jabbing the cell

155

phone at Drew, displaying it like a hand grenade. "Did you mention a certain boy on the Internet?"

"No! God, I'm not stupid."

"Debatable," Laurel said.

"Are you sure you didn't say anything about Kyle?" Mandy needed to know.

"Yes. I swear."

She was telling the truth. A wave of relief washed over Mandy as she slumped back in her chair. It wasn't so bad, not nearly as bad as it could have been.

"I'm sorry," Drew said. "I really am. I just thought you guys made such a great couple and everything, and Jacob and I are so happy, I want you to be happy too."

"I can be happy without a boyfriend," Mandy told her.

"Amen," Laurel said.

"How?" Drew asked.

After school, Mandy waited out front for Laurel. She stood by the school sign, leaning against the concrete post it hung on, wondering what was taking her friend so long. She decided to call and pulled her cell phone from her jacket. She looked at the device with a bit of fear. What if she tried to call Laurel and got a wrong number again? The same wrong number? The memory of crumpling paper static and that rasping voice unnerved her, and she thought about putting the phone away. But she couldn't let one bizarre accident, probably a crossed signal, rule her life. It was just a coincidence she happened to be in front of the library, alone and in the dark, when the call went through.

CUL8R

She hit Laurel's number on the speed dial and waited, heart pounding.

"I know," Laurel said instead of *hello*. "Still waiting for Mrs. Jacob Lurie to get out of the bathroom. She's probably slappin' on a new pad or something."

"Leave her," Mandy suggested.

"Would if I could. She's got my bio book. Don't ask. Long story. I'll be right out."

"Okay."

A horn beeped behind her, and Mandy turned to see Dale sitting in his Audi. He lifted a hand in a half wave.

"Need a ride?"

Mandy smiled and shook her head. "I'm waiting for Laurel."

"Cool," he said. Then he looked into the

rearview mirror, checked the road over his shoulder, and unbuckled his seat belt. A minute later, he was jogging over the grass toward her.

"What are you doing?" Mandy asked through a smile of confusion.

"I was gonna call," he said. "I mean, I want to call. Is it okay if I call you? Like around seven or something?"

He looked so nervous, so cute. Mandy had to laugh. "Yeah. That'd be nice."

"Cool," Dale said. Then he repeated, "Cool," before turning and jogging back to his car.

"What did I just see?" Laurel asked a moment later, walking up to her at the sign.

"Nothing," Mandy said.

"Didn't look like nothing to me."

As seven o'clock approached, Mandy sat in her room. To her surprise, Kyle's name appeared on her buddy list. *You're supposed to be in California,* she thought before realizing he probably was.

Everybody had laptops these days, and he said he was always online. She couldn't imagine going to someplace new like that and sitting in front of the computer. It was probably warm there. She'd want to walk around and see things. See everything. What a total waste to travel halfway across the country just to sit in a room and look at the same screen you could see at home.

Whatever, she thought.

She turned on her away message and leaned back in the chair, looking at the cell phone sitting on her desk. It was nearly seven, and she needed to be ready for Dale's call. Things like this demanded preparation.

She decided not to pick up on the first ring. That would be lame. She probably wouldn't pick up on the second ring either. In fact, she might let it go to voice mail and then call him back. But that was lame, too.

When the phone trilled, she decided to wait for the third ring.

"Hey," she said.

"Hey. How's it going?"

"Good. Just doing some homework."

"Tell me about it," Dale said. "I've got a bunch of pages to read for Stahlman tomorrow."

Then, there was a long silence. Mandy's nerves jangled, and she just couldn't sit there any longer.

So she stood up and started pacing, trying to figure out something to say.

"Laurel still there?" Dale asked.

"No, we just walked home together. She didn't come over."

"Oh," he said. "You're kind of quiet."

"Don't really know what to say."

"Me either," Dale admitted. "It's weird, right?"

"Yeah, kind of," Mandy said, completing a lap. She noticed someone had instant messaged her, even though her away message was on.

Kyle, she thought. It had to be him.

She stared at the screen, wondering if she should kill the away message. With the awkward silences between her and Dale, she almost wanted to. Maybe Kyle had news about college, or wanted to talk about their date Saturday night. Of course, it might not be him at all. Drew and Laurel IMed all the time. Mandy returned to the chair and reached for the mouse, pausing when Dale finally spoke.

"It's like all of this stuff is running through my head, but I don't know what to say first. We always used to have such great conversations, and now, I can't even get a sentence out, and it's just too weird. You know what I mean? I've got a bunch of stuff in my head, but it's all stupid, and all I want is for things to be the way they were."

Mandy bit down on her lower lip. She pulled her hand away from the mouse.

"So do I," she said.

Mimi's was the finest restaurant in Elmwood. Mandy's parents celebrated anniversaries at Mimi's and everyone else spoke about it with great reverence, but Mandy had never dined there before, never seen the romantic red walls and the lily-shaped crystal light sconces. The scarlet walls and carpet ate much of the light cast by these fixtures and the tiny flickering tabletop candles. Following Dale through the elegant room, she felt underdressed. Oh, her black dress was beautiful and it had cost quite a bit, but she still didn't think it appropriate for the amazing restaurant. She couldn't imagine anything she owned being appropriate for this place.

After school the day before, she and Dale had

gone to Corey's for coffee and chatted, mending some of the damage that had been done, and he'd suggested they go out for a nice dinner. Speaking to him on the phone Tuesday night had been awkward, even after they'd both said how much they missed each other. But yesterday at Corey's had been better, and tonight looked like it was going to be simply incredible.

Dale looked stunning in his gray suit and blue silk shirt. *Just like a movie star*, Mandy thought, unable to manage the jitters of excitement in her stomach. She felt certain that everyone was staring at her. Additionally, she was afraid she might trip and fall on her face or bump into something. Everything was just so perfect.

Once the maître d' seated them, Dale unfolded his napkin and dropped it into his lap. "Is this okay?" he asked.

"Okay?" Mandy asked. "It's wonderful."

"Cool," Dale said. "I mean, we never came here before, and I thought you might like it."

"I love it. But how did you get a reservation? Isn't it booked through the next millennium?"

"Just weekends," he said. "School nights aren't all that hard to book."

"You come here a lot?" Mandy asked. *And if so, why is this the first time you're bringing me here?*

"My dad likes the trout," Dale said. "We come out here every few weeks, so they kind of know me. I don't mention it much, because people already think I'm a spoiled ass." He laughed. "Anyway, if you like shrimp, the scampi is good. I guess everything is good. Just get what you want. Next time it's back to burgers and fries."

"The shrimp sounds nice," Mandy said, gazing over the table at Dale. He looked even more handsome in the flickering candlelight, more mature somehow.

"You look really beautiful," he told her. He reached over the table and took her hand. "Really," he said.

"Thank you."

When the waiter arrived to take their orders, he called Dale, "Master Dale," which made him scowl and blush. Mandy giggled, but got it under control quickly, seeing how self-conscious Dale felt. Though she scanned the menu a dozen times (and everything looked sooo good), she ordered the scampi.

After the waiter left them, they fell into an easy conversation, talking about school and their friends. Soon, Mandy forgot about the elegant room and thoughts of her inadequate dress, and just enjoyed speaking with Dale. He seemed to have changed so much in the last few weeks. His jokes weren't as crude, and he actually seemed to be listening when she spoke.

"So, you three are just going to fly off to Brazil after graduation?" Dale asked.

"Not necessarily Brazil. We could end up in Europe. I haven't even talked it over with them yet, but we may not all go to the same college. Then, who knows what's going to happen to us? We should have some kind of great memory together, you know?"

"Sure," he said, though he didn't seem convinced. "What brought all of this up?"

"Nicki mostly," Mandy said. Of course, she couldn't mention her chats with Kyle. "I was thinking about all the things she won't get to do. Then, I started thinking about everything I wanted to do."

Dale nodded his head, looked at his plate. "I guess we've all done a lot of thinking since that night. The first thing I noticed when we got back to school was how nice everyone was being, right? Everyone was kind of quiet and really polite. And I got that, because I felt the same way. The thing is, it's only been two weeks and school is getting back to normal, like everyone is mostly over it and the kids are acting like themselves again."

This observation seemed to worry Dale. Mandy thought she knew why. He didn't want to be the way he was before Nicki's death. He'd discovered things about himself and his family, and it really changed him. Now though, he was concerned the change was only temporary. She reached out and took his hand, squeezing it tightly.

"She was online that night," Dale said. "Before that bastard kidnapped her, she was online. I saw her on my buddy list."

Thinking about Dale on the computer that night stung Mandy. She remembered far too clearly what he was doing. Still, she didn't remember Nicki being signed on, though by the time she got home to her own computer and buddy list, her fight with Dale was the only thing in her head.

"I always considered my list like a kind of party," Dale said. "I could just hang out and chat, and it's like all of my friends were right there, all the time, watching out for each other and having a good time. But Nicki was there, surrounded by all of us, and then she was just gone."

Mandy held his hand tighter. She didn't know what to say. She certainly was not going to bring up Kyle and how she told herself he wasn't real just because she only knew him through lines of text. That was the last thing they needed tonight.

"Wow, that killed the conversation," Dale said, letting loose another nervous laugh. "Let's find something a little less Poe to talk about."

"Well," Mandy said, "are you doing anything cool this weekend?"

"I don't know," Dale said. "Are we?"

They stood on Mandy's porch, kissing. As always, Dale held her just tight enough, and from his lips and tongue a tingling charge filled Mandy, who held the back of his head, fearing he might pull away. Their date had been perfect, like something out of a movie. She hated that they had school in the morning, hated that it was only eleven o'clock and they were saying good night. She crushed her lips to his, forgetting that her parents might open the door any second. The kiss seemed to go on forever, yet it still ended too soon.

"I'll pick you up in the morning," Dale said.

Mandy nodded, not yet able to speak. He kissed her again, a quick peck on the lips.

"Good night," he said.

"'Night," she managed.

She watched him walk back to his car, saw him climb in behind the wheel. He waved good night, and she waved back. Then, Dale pulled away, leaving Mandy trembling with exhilaration, fumbling for her house keys.

Upstairs in her room, Mandy looked at her computer. She probably had a ton of e-mails from Drew and Laurel. Both had insisted she call or IM the second she got home to download the details of her date, but she wanted to keep this feeling to herself for a while, felt like holding it close and tight so it wasn't lost. Instead of signing on, she shut the machine down.

Mandy changed into a nightshirt with a picture of a lamb on the front and lay on her bed. Against the dimly lit ceiling, she replayed her date, seeing Dale in his nice gray suit, and the restaurant with its waiters dressed in tuxedos. It was all so wonderful.

Things were back to the way they should be.

Except for Kyle, she thought. She still had to chat with him, needed to cancel their date for Saturday night. She couldn't go out with him now, and he probably wouldn't want to chat anymore once he knew Mandy had a boyfriend. The whole mess made her feel queasy. It would be easier to just send him an e-mail, but that was lame. He'd be back from California tomorrow. After school, she would explain things. She knew he'd understand.

Then everything really would be back to normal.

In Friday morning gym class, Laurel tried to get as much information as she could between Mr. Lombard's instructions on Tae Kwan Do techniques. Mandy was still high from the date and wanted to tell Laurel everything, but knew it would have to wait until lunch. In the meantime, she let out a few juicy details—about Dale, about their dinner—just to drive Laurel nuts.

In the cafeteria, once Drew joined them, she told her friends everything, starting with Dale's phone call after school telling her to dress up, then about arriving at Mimi's and feeling like a total looz in her dress. She told them about the restaurant and the food and the conversation and the kiss good night. At first, Drew interrupted a lot, wanting to talk about similar moments she and Jacob shared. After Laurel threatened to make her eat her own hair, Drew quieted.

"And you think the leopard really changed his spots?" Laurel asked.

"I do," Mandy said. "I can't explain it, but Nicki's dying really affected him. He's romantic and sweet, but he's still Dale, you know?"

"Sounds like we have a winner," Laurel said. "Now, what about voting the other one off the island o' Mandy?"

"Ugh," Mandy said. "I know. I'm doing it tonight after school."

"What are you going to tell him?" Drew asked.

"The truth."

"Never a good idea," Laurel said. "But it's your life. Do what you have to."

That night, Mandy stared at her buddy list, more specifically at Kyle's username. *I so don't want to do this,* she thought. *How am I supposed to just say 'Hi, I never want to chat with you again'?* Uncomfortable, Mandy shifted in her chair and took a deep breath. *Just like a bandage. It's better to yank and get it over with.*

MC9010025: Hey. Are U back?

No, Mandy thought, *don't use webspeak*. She wanted Kyle to know that she was serious and using a bunch of symbols in place of words would look lame, like it was just another stupid chat.

Kylenevers: Back. Glad 2 b home.
MC9010025: That's good.
Kylenevers: I had a great idea.
MC9010025: What's that?
Kylenevers: Well, we're getting together tomorrow night, right?
MC9010025: Kyle, we have to chat about something.
Kylenevers: Plenty of time 4 that. I was thinking we'd have dinner in the park. U know, kind of a moonlight picnic.
MC9010025: That sounds really nice, Kyle. But I can't
Kylenevers: What do u mean? Don't u want to meet?
MC9010025: My boyfriend and I got back together. I was trying to tell you.
Kylenevers: Oh. U never mentioned a

boyfriend.

MC9010025: We broke up. Long story. But we're back together now.

Kylenevers: K

MC9010025: No, it's not okay. I feel terrible about this

Kylenevers: We'll still meet

MC9010025: You don't understand, Kyle. I can't.

Kylenevers: U don't want 2 hurt him

MC9010025: No.

Kylenevers: But it's ok 2 hurt me?

MC9010025: I don't want to hurt you.

Kylenevers: What if I want 2 hurt u?

MC9010025: Don't say that.

Kylenevers: Why not?

MC9010025: Because you're just mad right now. You're angry at me because of all of this, but it will pass. You hardly know me.

Kylenevers: That's not true. I know ur smart

MC9010025: Thnx

Kylenevers: And funny

MC9010025: Kyle don't. I feel awful

Kylenevers: And warm.

MC9010025: I don't feel very warm right now.

Kylenevers: Sure u do. When I slice open your belly and stick my hands inside, I'm sure you'll feel very warm. And then you'll get cold, as cold as the night air. But I'll keep cutting.

Mandy jerked away from the monitor as if the text tried to lunge out and grab her throat. A high squeal leaped behind her lips, and she struggled to keep from screaming. It was a joke. A sick joke. It had to be. She reached toward the keyboard with trembling fingers.

MC9010025: That's not funny.

Kylenevers: Nicki didn't think so either, but I think it's hilarious. Hahahahahahahahahahahahahahahahahah ahahahahahaha . . .

Now Mandy did scream. She shoved away from the desk, stumbling over the chair as she tried to put distance between herself and the monitor. Her mind raced. Her heart fluttered like a hummingbird's wings against her ribs. *No. No. No,* she thought. It couldn't be Kyle. The man that killed Nicki was old, stooped and grotesque. She saw him on the video. Everyone saw him. A man with a witch's face. Kyle looked nothing like him, and the picture must have come from Kyle. He posed for her exactly as she asked, with the hairbrush, saluting. He was young and handsome and . . . the picture changed. No. Pictures don't just change. No way.

"No," she cried to the room.

A cold chill clung to her skin like an icy rash. She trembled violently beneath it. *Call help*, she thought. *Figure this out later, but for now, call help. You're alone in the house.*

Mandy approached the desk as she might a hive of bees. Slow steps brought her shaking to the edge. She snatched the cell phone from the desk, then leaped back. She fumbled the device open and punched in 911, then hit send and put the phone to her ear.

"Still want to chat on the phone?" a high rasping voice asked. Then a piercing stutter erupted through the speaker. "Hahahahahahahahahahaha."

She screamed and threw the phone across the

room, repulsed by the laughter crawling through it. Her skin tightened and goose-pimpled. Mandy hugged herself against the sensation, but she felt dirty, as if she'd just squirmed out of the Witchman's filthy embrace.

Mandy looked around the bedroom, uncertain what to do. She tried to get her heartbeat under control by taking deep, ragged breaths. Tears burned her eyes, blurred her vision. She wiped the hot tears away frantically so she could see.

Get out of the house, she told herself. *Go to a neighbor's, use their phone. If Kyle knows my cell number, he probably knows my home number and my address!*

What if I want 2 hurt u?

Oh God, she thought. Mandy sprinted from the bedroom and into the hall. She hit the stairs running, flying blindly down them, her only thought to get someplace else, someplace safe. She slid on the tiles, slowing herself to unlock the front door. Her fingers slipped on the deadbolt handle. Slipped again. Finally, it turned and she grasped the knob, threw the door open, and raced forward, right into his arms.

"Mandy," Dale said. "Mandy. Hey, come on. Calm down. It's just me."

Struggling blindly against the guy holding her, not yet able to see Dale where she'd seen Kyle only moments before, Mandy threw an arm out and hit her boyfriend's shoulder as hard as she could.

"Hey!" Dale yelped, shaking her hard until she was really seeing him. "Hey," he said, his voice quieter, soothing. "It's me."

Recognition settled over her. Relieved to be held by familiar and welcomed hands, Mandy stopped struggling. More than anything, she just wanted to fall into his arms and be held until the fear passed, but there was no time.

"Come on," she said, pulling out of Dale's grasp. She turned and closed the front door. "We have to go."

Dale looked concerned, but he wasn't ready to move just yet. His instinct to protect her had kicked in, and he looked ready for a fight. "Go where? What's going on? Is someone in your house?"

"No, it's just . . ."

Mandy took more deep breaths and shook her

hands before her to break out the last of the panic. Dale was here. She wasn't alone, and that was something. He had his cell phone. Kyle wouldn't have that number; there would be no way for him to have it. She never mentioned Dale by name in their chats. They could call the police and wait together.

Inside, Mandy realized that Dale might be hurt if she told him the truth. She had, after all, chatted with Kyle for weeks. Dale would take that as cheating, but she couldn't worry about that right now. If he hadn't been doing the same thing, Mandy never would have replied to Kyle.

"I have to tell you something," Mandy said. "But I'm not sure I know how."

Still, she found a way. A moment later, the story of how she met Kyle and why she replied to him in the first place came pouring out of her mouth. When she saw a cloud of anger fall over Dale's face, she talked faster, explaining that she and the boy never met, never even spoke on the phone. "Now that we're back together, I told him I couldn't chat with him anymore."

Dale nodded his head, still looking hurt and angry. "So, what did he say?"

"Come on," Mandy said. "I'll show you."

She led him up the stairs. "At first, he was really cool, we just chatted about what was happening, you know, ever since Nicki was killed. He was always a little weird, but I felt bad for him, because he told me his parents were really strict and a bunch of other stuff." As they walked into her bedroom, Mandy paused and turned to Dale. "And I was upset because *we* weren't together, you know?"

Dale nodded his head, let Mandy kiss him. His eyes were cold. He understood, but that didn't mean he had to be happy about it.

"Then tonight," Mandy said, taking Dale's hand and leading him to the monitor, "He wrote . . ."

They stared at a blank screen. At first, Mandy thought her screen saver was on. She tapped the return key. Hit it harder.

"No," she said. "I didn't shut this down."

"Are you sure?" Dale asked. "You were pretty upset."

"I'm sure," she said, seeing her reflection in the dark panel. She really jabbed at the return key, giving it a solid click. Nothing. "How?"

Without the instant message from Kyle, she had no proof. It was her word against his. *No wait*, she thought. *The cell phone call.* Mandy pulled away from Dale and skirted her bed, rushing to the far corner where her cell phone lay closed. Mandy picked up the device, opened it, and searched her log for the last incoming call.

The last call logged to her cell phone came from Laurel that morning. No other incoming calls, or outgoing calls—not even her 911 call was listed.

"This isn't possible," Mandy said. She turned to Dale, who stood by the desk. "When I tried to call the police, he was on the line."

"You gave him your cell phone number?" Dale asked. "I thought you said you guys never talked on the phone?"

"We didn't. I never gave him the number. I don't know how he got it."

She could tell by his expression that Dale didn't believe her. Though it hurt, she was more worried about finding something solid she could take to the police. The only thing left was the picture. She sat in the chair at her desk, powered up her computer, nervously gnawing her thumbnail. Dale stood glowering over her.

"Don't you think it's kind of stupid to start up a conversation with some guy right after Nicki got killed? I mean, you never know who you're chatting with."

"I know. That's why I made him send me a very specific picture of himself, so I'd know it was just taken and not a phony."

"Where's the picture?"

"I'll show you as soon as this thing comes on."

It took forever—the screen glowed and icons began popping up, but it all seemed to be happening very slowly. When it finally loaded, Mandy guided her cursor to the file with Kyle's picture and clicked. She was horrified when the window opened.

"God, Mandy," Dale said, the anger clear in his voice. "What the hell were you thinking? The guy looks forty years old."

Mandy stared at the picture, wondering if she was losing her mind. Dale was right; the man in the photograph did look forty years old, nothing like the boy who once saluted her. The man still saluted, but now his face sagged. Wrinkles scored his eyes and mouth. His nose was larger. Where Kyle's neatly brushed blond hair was, now sprouted tufts nearly gray. His embarrassed expression had also hardened, and now he looked amused but cruel. In his hand, he still held something, but it no longer resembled a hair-brush, just a black smudge, like thick smoke, hovering over something with a sharp, silver edge.

"I don't believe this," Dale said. "Was being with me so bad you had to go chasing Grandpa Munster?"

Mandy shouted, "He didn't look like this! The picture is changing!"

"Yeah," Dale said. "That happens all the time."

"Dammit, Dale. I'm not lying. Drew and Laurel both saw this just last week. They'll tell you he didn't look like this."

"Look, whatever," he said. "The guy threatened you. Let's call the cops and get this over with."

But what was Mandy going to tell them? It all seemed so impossible: no cell phone record; no instant message; her computer shutting down on its own; a picture of a guy her father's age, someone she had no business chatting with in the first place. Who was going to believe her? They'd think she deserved what was happening to her for being so stupid.

She knew she had to call the police, but the ache in her stomach kicked painfully, assuring her that the next few hours were going to be miserable.

Mandy sat in her desk chair and looked up at Officer Romero, who stood straight-backed, wearing an expression that revealed no discernible emotion. Dale waited downstairs at the request of the police officer, leaving Mandy attempting to explain a series of bizarre events that revolved around a boy named Kyle.

"That picture," Officer Romero said. "Did it come attached to an e-mail?"

"Yes," Mandy said, with a sudden rush of relief. The e-mail. She'd forgotten about it completely. That would be some kind of proof, some real connection to Kyle. It would help them find him; they could trace something like that.

She searched her mail folders, plugged in the

e-mail address as she remembered it, but came up with nothing. It had to be there. She must have remembered the addy wrong. Instead of trying another search, she scrolled through her saved mail. Nothing.

"Wait, I wrote back to him," she said feeling insecure under the intense eyes of Officer Romero. But a thorough search of her sent mail uncovered nothing. Notes to Drew and Laurel and a dozen other people, but nothing to Kyle.

"This can't be," she whispered. "I swear I'm telling you the truth."

Officer Romero nodded her head. Her face softened. "Calm down, Mandy. We have the username you gave us. I'm going to take down the e-mail address as you remember it. It's possible he gained access to your mail service. If he already had your screen name, it would just be an issue of working out your password. We'll check with the provider. Even if he managed to get in and erase his tracks, they'll have a record."

"Thank you," Mandy said, relieved. "I thought I was going crazy."

"You're not crazy," Officer Romero said. "And I don't want you to upset yourself. I think what we have here is a hack trying to scare you."

"But he mentioned Nicki."

"I know. It's mean and it's sick, but it would be highly unlikely for the real perpetrator to admit to the crime, not when you have everything we need to trace him."

"And you didn't find anything on Nicki's computer?" Mandy asked. "I mean, what if *she* was in touch with this guy?"

"Unlikely," Officer Romero said. "It's procedure to run cell phone and Internet records. Everything of Nicolette's checked out. I'm not saying that we won't treat this like a real threat or a real crime, because it is. I'm just telling you not to upset yourself too much. That doesn't mean you should take any chances. I wouldn't walk anywhere on your own, and make sure you're with friends if you're out in the evenings. Also, this guy may try to contact you again. If he does, log the time and what was said and call me immediately."

"I will. But, Officer Romero, I still don't understand what's happening with the picture. It keeps changing. Is it some kind of program that just looks like a jpeg file?"

"Maybe. I'm not a computer wiz, so I don't

know how all of these things work. I'll need you to print out a copy of the image for me, though. Let's also send the file to my e-mail and I'll have one of our tech guys examine it."

Mandy reached across her desk and pushed the button, turning on her printer. Then, she looked at the image of Kyle, now a middle-aged man, and felt the familiar, cold fingers of fear on her neck and spine. She sent the image to print, then closed the file. After she had e-mailed the image to Romero's office addy, Mandy pulled the printed image from the tray.

"Oh no," she said.

In the middle of the white sheet of paper was a black square with a narrow gray line down the center. No Kyle, young or old, no hairbrush, no room appeared at all.

"I don't understand," Mandy said.

"That makes two of us," said Officer Romero.

After Officer Romero left, Mandy turned off her cell phone. She signed off the Internet, then shut her computer down completely. Once, these devices had represented a connection to her friends, an invisible thread to keep them together no matter how many miles separated them. They were gateways to the world and its people, conversation, and fun. Now they scared her, because among the welcomed and known people in her life was Kyle, unwelcome and unknown. As she severed the pathways Kyle used to find her, Dale hovered at her shoulder, standing like a bodyguard. Finally, Mandy's mother came home. Then her father. Dale told her he had to get home for dinner.

At the door, after kissing her good night, he said, "I'll come by later. We'd better just stay in tonight." Mandy nodded her head and kissed him again.

Over dinner, Mandy explained her situation to her parents, told them about Kyle and Officer Romero's visit. Her father looked at her like she'd just told him she was pregnant. Her mother, always intent on being so understanding, dropped her fork on the plate and leaned on the table, resting her chin on her hands.

"And when were you going to tell us about this boy?" Mrs. Collins asked angrily.

"We haven't even met. We were just chatting. It was no big deal."

"Apparently, it was," her mother said. "The police were here. You didn't even bother to tell us you'd broken up with Dale."

"So?" Mandy asked. "What does that have to do with anything?"

Her mother shot a quick glance at her father, who had said little up to that point. His sturdy round face wore an expression of disappointment and disgust, and Mrs. Collins gave him the floor.

"Mandy," he said, scratching the day's growth of stubble on his chin. "If we don't know what's going on in your life, we can't really do our jobs. I'd say we've given you plenty of room. We don't ask a lot of questions or make a lot of rules. But that's going to have to change now."

"Dad," Mandy said. "Dale and I are supposed to . . ."

"I'm speaking," he warned, his voice low and controlled. "You're nearly an adult. Pretty soon, you'll be out on your own making a lot of the same mistakes your mother and I did when we were your age. But until then, it is our job to protect you, which means knowing what's going on in your life. After dinner, I want you to run up and get me your cell phone. I'm going to have to change the number anyway, apparently. You'll get it back in two weeks. Until then, you're grounded."

"Dad!" Mandy said. "You can't punish me for being a victim."

"You're not a victim, and we aren't going to let you be one," her mother said, nearly in tears. "We are not going to go through what Nicolette's parents went through. We are not going to wait while the police search for your body. We are not going to stand up on a stage and cry our hearts out because we were so afraid our little girl would hate us that we didn't protect her. I don't want you on that cell phone, and I don't want you online."

"So, I'm just supposed to ignore my friends for two weeks?"

"They can visit you here," her father said. "You can use the house phone. That's it."

"I don't believe this."

"After dinner, I'm going to call Officer Romero and see if there are any other precautions we should be taking. I'm pretty pissed off she didn't bother to call us. Also, if you have a picture of this man, we want to see it."

———————

". . . and, it's like I already turned the phone off and shut the computer down," Mandy told Laurel over the clunky plastic phone her dad installed in her room. "I'm not stupid, but God, to forbid me from going online for two weeks? I'll have like a billion e-mails."

"Don't tell my dad, or we'll both be land-locked."

"They'd better catch this ass."

"Did he really say he was going to cut you?"

"Yes."

"And he mentioned Nicki?"

"Yes."

"Then you better do what you're told," Laurel said. "And I'm thinking that after my target practice tomorrow, I ought to swing by your place with a present."

"The gun?"

"That's right."

"No way," Mandy said. "I don't even know how to work one."

"It's easy. You shoot the fast thing into the slow thing."

"Uh . . . no. Thanks. My dad's already been climbing up Officer Romero's butt, so now we have a police car cruising our block."

"Are they hotties?"

"Laurel!"

"I'm just playin'. Look, five-oh has this guy's stats. These days, it takes like two minutes to trace that kind of info. It's probably just some clown with a tiny unit looking for giggles, but you just don't know, right? I'm not usually down with parental guidance. This time, I say let 'em lead. Lie low. It'll probably all be over tomorrow."

"I hope so."

Mandy didn't sleep well. How could she? As she lay in bed, her mind was filled with rambling voices and frightening lines of text.

> What if I want 2 hurt u? . . . When I slice open your belly and stick my hands inside, I'm sure you'll feel very warm. Nicki didn't think so either, but I think it's hilarious. Hahaha . . . CUL8R.

She pictured the Witchman, threats spilling from his thin lips like a black cloud. His cackling laugh cut through her mind. Kyle appeared, looking older and cruel, saluting her with a palm stretched over wild animal eyes. Every car that rolled down the street, every rustle of bush and whisper of wind outside was Kyle coming for her. A board creaked in the hallway, and Mandy's heart leaped into her throat before she heard her mother's voice, speaking quietly to her father. When sleep came, she dreamed of the terrible wooded place where the Witchman stalked her and kids sat at misty computers, typing, always typing. Then he was in her room. He crouched like a gargoyle on the end of her bed, his black coat pooling over her comforter like a bloodstain. Motionless, he hunched on the covers with his beaklike nose and his pointed chin. His eyes were as narrow as slits.

Mandy thought she woke up then, but the monitor of her computer glowed like a ghostly window. It must be part of the dream. It had to be. Mandy squeezed her eyes closed in terror. When she opened them again, the screen was dark.

She was awake when the dawn came. Grim light filtered through her bedroom window, which suddenly reminded her of a giant computer screen. Groggy, she rolled over and stared at the nightstand, the clunky phone atop it.

CUL8R

Mandy began to cry. The tears came out of nowhere, scaring her with their intensity. She felt totally cut off and alone. She covered her face and let the tears come, let the stinging tears burn her eyes and cheeks. This wasn't real. She hadn't done anything wrong.

"I didn't do anything," she whimpered into her palms. Then something Laurel said pounded loudly in her head.

Now, you think someone is playing you, and you figure it's got to be someone that has a reason to be playin'. I'm just sayin' that some folks don't need a reason. Some folks get their giggle on just knowin' you're scared, whether they know you or not.

Life couldn't be that random, Mandy thought. It just couldn't. If it were, then she would never be safe, not truly safe. And again, Laurel's words were there to knock away her protest with a harsh philosophy, one directed at Drew during Nicki's candlelight vigil.

Psychos aren't interested in morality plays. They hunt and they slice and it's usually the innocent that take the blade. . . . And if you think being all innocent and sweet is gonna protect you from anything, then take a good look around, because the next one of these is yours.

"No, it's not," Mandy said, sniffling loudly. She took her hands from her eyes, wiped the tears away. She wasn't going to be just another victim, another yearbook photo for the nightly news anchor to pretend to care about. Determined to protect herself, Mandy scrubbed the remainder of her tears away and sat up in the bed.

Across the room, her monitor glowed. Suddenly, icons began to pop up on her wallpaper.

"Oh God," she whispered before running from the room.

Mandy sat with a cup of coffee, her back to the only wall in the kitchen that didn't have windows. When she heard her parents walking down the stairs, she lifted the knife from the table and returned it to the holder on the counter. She thought of the gun Laurel had offered, wishing she'd said yes, but knew the knife would have to do for now. She'd sneak it upstairs later once her parents were busy. Her parents greeted her with sleepy "mornings" and poured themselves coffee. They didn't look as angry. In fact, their expressions were soft and understanding. They took turns kissing her on the cheek.

"Sleep okay?" her father asked.

"Yes," she lied.

"You look like you were up all night," her mother said.

"Thanks a lot."

"I'm allowed to be worried. Did you really sleep?"

"I'm fine, mom."

At ten-thirty, Officer Romero called. She didn't have good news.

"The file you sent me crashed my system," she said. "Our support people are going through it now, but they think there was a virus attached to the picture. It might have infected your e-mail, which is how this guy was able to access your files."

"What about the username and e-mail address?" Mandy asked.

"Nothing yet, but it's the weekend. Nobody moves very fast. I'm sure we'll have something soon. How are you holding up?"

Mandy looked around the kitchen to make sure her parents weren't near and said, "I'm scared."

"It's okay to be scared," Officer Romero told her. "But the more I think about this, the more I believe we just have a geek with a sick sense of humor."

"I hope you're right," Mandy said.

"We'll keep a car in your neighborhood. You hang in there."

"Thank you. I will."

Mandy hung up the phone. She stared at it, expecting it to ring, expecting Kyle to be on the other end taunting her. When that didn't happen, she pulled the big kitchen knife from the holder, held it close to her side, so she could hide it if her parents surprised her in the hall, then went up to her room.

She stepped inside, her eyes immediately drawn to the monitor. The swirls and lines of her screen saver played over the screen. Leaving her door open, Mandy went to the bed and slid the knife under her pillow.

At her computer, she killed the screen saver and looked at Kyle's picture file. *What do you look like now?* she wondered, her hand hovering over the mouse.

He was even older. His hair now completely white and jutting from his head in wisps like the fluff of a cotton ball. The nose was bigger, the wrinkles deeper. *A virus,* she thought. *An advanced program masked as a jpeg.*

She wanted to delete the image, just double click it into oblivion, but Mandy knew she couldn't. Officer Romero might need her to send it again, or else the police might send computer experts to examine her system. It was the only real evidence they had.

In an act of defiance, refusing to completely give in to her fear, Mandy left the image open. It would remind her to be scared, remind her to be careful.

Sitting on her bed, she lifted the handset of the clunky phone and dialed Laurel's cell number. It went directly to voice mail, and Mandy remembered her friend was at "gun school." She left a message, insisting Laurel call as soon as she could. Then, she called Drew, but she couldn't talk because she was at Corey's with Jacob having pancakes.

"Call me later. It's important."

"I will. Swear to God."

Finally, she called Dale. His father answered the phone, his voice gruff with annoyance. Mandy remembered what Dale said about him being so unhappy and, for a flicker of a moment, she wondered what else the man could want. But then Dale was on the phone.

"You okay?" he asked. He didn't sound angry or hurt anymore. That was good.

"Didn't sleep very well," she admitted.

"Me either. I don't think I slept at all."

"Can you come over?" Mandy asked. "I think I'd really like to have you here right now."

"Is that cool with your parents?"

"Sure. I mean, I think so. They said I could have friends over."

"Okay," he said. "But I have to do some things around here first. Dad is having a particularly asslike day. It might be an hour or two. Is that cool?"

"As soon as you can," Mandy said.

Back at the computer, she saw that the picture had changed again. She'd only been on the phone for less than three minutes, but already, the white tufts of hair were thinner. The eyes narrower. The dark smudge, where a hairbrush had been, was fading. She could almost make out an object, silver and metallic, beneath. She looked away, out the window. When she looked back, the picture had changed again.

"It can't be," she said.

She saw it then, the resemblance to another face. Before, he had hid behind youth, but now that façade was crumbling away.

It was a face she'd seen on a news broadcast. The face she'd stared at in horror after Laurel downloaded his image from the Web. The face of the man in her dreams. The Witchman.

"I've never heard of anything like this," Laurel said. "I'll give it to the freak, he's got skills."

"Yeah," Mandy said nervously, twirling the phone cord around her finger. "Let's all compliment my personal psycho."

"Sorry, M."

"No, it's okay. I'm just creeped out, but the police are circling the neighborhood. My parents refuse to leave the house, and Dale will be here in a few minutes."

"What's he look like now?" Laurel asked.

Mandy looked at the screen, at the picture of the man. Thinner hair. Nose more pronounced than ever. Chin pointed. A slightly younger version of the Witchman she'd seen on the video scowled out at her from beneath a saluting hand. In his other hand where there was once a hairbrush, he held a long, narrow-bladed knife that caught a glimmer of light.

Ten minutes ago, when she was absolutely sure it was the same man, she called Officer Romero, whose computer was still out cold from the invading virus. Less than two minutes later, she saw a police car circling her block. The men didn't park or come in, which Mandy thought was odd, but Officer Romero assured her that she herself would be at Mandy's within the hour. By then, the traces on Kyle Nevers would be in.

"Hey," Laurel said. "You still there?"

"I'm here, just don't ask me about the picture again."

"So, how is this going to play? You need some company tonight?"

"Yes," Mandy said. "But I can't have it. The police don't want too many people wandering around the house. They say it makes their job harder."

"Well, you know I'm there if you need me."

"I know," Mandy said. Then, before she knew it, she was saying, "I love you, L. I never tell you that, but you're a great friend."

"Love you, too, Girl. Be strong."

"I will," she said, and hung up the phone. It felt

like she was saying good-bye forever.

Mandy walked through the house, looking at the sleek furniture her mother adored, finally able to see some beauty in the hard smooth surfaces. Despite their cold appearance, they brought light to the rooms, bits of sun dancing off glass tables and the facets of crystal knick-knacks. She found her parents in the kitchen. Both were still drinking coffee. She hugged them tightly.

She was safe here, with her family. The doors were locked. Dale would be there soon. She was so very afraid, but she was also rational (Laurel always said so), and logic told her she was safe. She would go upstairs and lie down until Dale arrived—*Where are you?*—and they'd all wait together until the police called to say they'd caught the son of a bitch, and they could resume their normal lives.

"Keep your door open," her father reminded.

"I will."

And she did. Upstairs, she walked into her bedroom. Still really creeped out, she checked under her bed, looked through her closet to make sure no one broke in while she was in the kitchen.

Finding the room empty, she dropped onto her bed, exhausted but still buzzing from fear.

Her eyes were just closing when a tone from her computer announced new mail in her e-mail folder. She didn't care. It would still be there after her nap.

But you never signed on, a tiny voice reminded.

Mandy's eyes shot open and she leaped from the bed. Her Internet homepage covered the screen, and an instant message window was open in the corner.

Kylenevers: It's L8R now.

Panicked, Mandy closed the window and clicked on the pull down menu. She signed off of the Internet service. The pages vanished, leaving nothing but the open picture file in the middle of her monitor.

It had changed again.

She couldn't tell if the photo of the Witchman was fully realized or not, because he was gone, and so was the room he'd been standing in. Instead, Mandy looked at the image of a brightly lit lawn. Sprinklers soaked the grass in a gemlike cascade.

The image shook, and she realized it was no longer a photo at all, but rather a movie playing in the picture box.

Whoever held the camera taking this film had shaky hands. The edges of the scene blurred and trembled in a disquieting tremor. The camera panned up and Mandy saw a white fence and a stretch of sidewalk.

It looked so familiar, but she couldn't place it.

Then the image progressed, down the walk past the house. She saw rows of nice houses. The houses of her neighbors! *Oh no*, she thought. A police car slowly pulled into the frame, eased its way down the street. Her street!

Oh God, she thought. *He's coming.*

The movie progressed faster and the cameraman stood in her driveway, aiming the camera up at her window.

But the police are out there. They had to see him. This can't be today. Can't be now.

The cameraman walked forward and pushed open the front door of her house. The image swept across her living room, back to the stairs, to the den, back to the stairs. Whoever held the camera began to climb toward her room.

"No!" Mandy cried, running to the hall, looking at the stairs.

Only to find them empty.

"Mom. Dad!" she cried, but her throat was so tight with dread, hardly any sound escaped. She ran back through her room to look out the window.

The police car was still retreating down the block. Another car pulled up. A silver Audi. It turned into her driveway.

Thank God, Dale.

He climbed out of his car. Dale looked up at the window, saw Mandy, waved.

"He's a good kid," a raspy voice said at her back. "I should drop him a note sometime."

Mandy spun toward the voice, her heart tripping hard. Her throat clenched with fear.

The Witchman stood by her door, wearing a black coat and a vicious smile. Mandy screamed, and this time the sound was piercing, dreadful. Below, her parents called out for her, and she heard their steps pounding up the staircase. The Witchman slammed her bedroom door, turned the lock.

"Think you might want to kiss me?" he asked.

Mandy remembered the knife under her pillow and dashed to the bed, grabbing the handle and stepping back, brandishing it before her. The Witchman didn't seem to notice a thunder of fists on the door at his back. Her parents' concerned voices, calling her name, demanding she let them in.

"Open the door," Mandy said, jabbing the knife forward, stepping to the end of the bed. "He's in here," she screamed.

None of this seemed to affect the Witchman in the least. He stepped away from the door toward the desk.

Now, not even the bed separated them. The only obstacle between him and her was the blade of her knife.

He looked at her computer screen and laughed his terrible staccato laugh before turning his attention back to Mandy. She cast a quick glance at the monitor, saw herself brandishing a long knife.

"Why don't you stupid brats just delete the file?" he asked. "You leave the gate wide open."

"You came through the computer? It . . . it isn't possible."

"I've been doing the impossible for many, many years, Mandy. People see only what I want them to see. For generations I've been called warlock and sorcerer and bogeyman. But the world changes. So, I've gone high tech."

"Get out of here!" Mandy screamed.

"I'm afraid I can't. The fuel I need is inside you."

From the other side of the door, she heard Dale call her name. A heavy thud pounded against wood. Both of her parents were screaming with tears in their voices.

Something in Mandy snapped. She could no longer take the smug, evil amusement on the Witchman's face. She ran forward, drawing the knife down to deliver an upward slice. But he stepped to the side and grabbed her, holding her tight to his body, her arms pinned at her sides.

Up close, his face was even more horrible. Like old leather, cracked and dusty, his skin stretched over bumpy, pointed bones. His eyes were the charcoal gray of a dead computer screen. His grip was like iron.

"Time to go," he said.

No. Please no.

Suddenly, Mandy felt herself falling, as if the floor had just dropped out from beneath her. The pounding on the door, the screaming of Dale and her mom and her dad, faded and grew thick as if heard from beneath water. Her body began to tingle and then burn as she felt herself coming apart, every cell letting loose of those around it. She tried to scream, but all she heard was static, like the crumpling of a paper bag.

Then Mandy's room was empty. Against the wall stood her desk. On the desk, her computer monitor glowed. A picture box in the middle of the screen still played a movie, showing a police car parked next to a curb. The doors opened and two burly men in blue uniforms ran forward as if right through the camera, leaving the image of a pleasant neighborhood. A terrified face appeared for a moment and was then pushed aside by a pale, old hand, dotted with liver spots. It appeared again, eyes wide, mouth open and screaming. The girl in the movie was struggling, slapping at the camera, crying for her parents, crying for a boy named Dale.

Dale threw his shoulder against the door and the jamb splintered, snapped and exploded inward. He didn't see Mandy. He ran to the closet, threw it open, but it was empty. Her parents were already at the window, looking out.

"It's locked," her father said.

Dale crouched low and looked under the bed, but saw nothing except long plastic containers, where Mandy kept her sweaters. Standing up, he noticed the open picture window on Mandy's monitor. Two police officers burst into the room, their guns drawn.

"Where are they?" one shouted.

"I don't know," Mandy's father said, his voice tearful and trembling.

"Where's my daughter!" Mrs. Collins screamed.

At the computer, Dale leaned down to get a better vantage on the picture window. When he saw the image there, his stomach knotted and he felt like he was going to be sick.

"Oh, Mandy," he cried.

There is a picture on the screen. It is just a simple picture, harmless in and of itself, but it carries a dreadful power. The image is of the corner of a blond brick building. Next to the building is a field of tall dead grass; beyond that, a stand of trees, dark and impenetrable despite the glow of bright afternoon sun.

EPILOGUE

Anne laughed, or more rightly, cackled. After a moment, Shirley joined in, showing her white teeth. The lively sounds echoed against the wounded plaster and peeling paint, rising above the rumble of the storm to fill the gloomy room with noise. Pieces of old wood ticked and settled as if the laughter itself had moved the building just a bit.

Finally Mary stood up, annoyed.

"That was awful!" she said, forgetting to whisper. "There was no point! No moral! No spiritual substance. That poor girl died like an animal. Like a rat in a cage."

Shirley clasped her hand to her mouth to stop her giggles, but her eyes caught Anne's and she started to guffaw again.

"That's enough," Daphne cautioned.

"Check the stats, Mary," Anne said, dark eyes glowing in the lantern flame. "We all die like animals. You're just a big rat. A big blond rat with curls."

Then she started laughing again.

But Mary was upset. "Are you that dead inside?"

"Inside and out," Anne said, leading to another round of harsh laughter.

"Aren't you even disappointed it wasn't your story?"

Anne waved her off. "Not. I don't expect it to be anymore. I just roll the dice and talk the talk. It's no PlayStation, but what is?"

As their voices rose, Daphne began shushing them in earnest. "Quiet down now, all of you. That's enough."

Shirley exhaled and turned her head sideways to look at the bones. She whispered, "Do you think maybe, even if they're not ours, the story that comes to us has *something* to do with us? With who we are? Anne is the darkest of us, no offense."

"Yeah, because I've been dating so much recently," Anne said.

Mary shook her head and also spoke softly as

211

she repeated her earlier theory. "The only pattern we know is the one that wins. The rest is just guessing."

"Like rats in a maze," Anne said. She let out another noisy laugh and buried her head in her hands to stifle the sound. Hearing that, Shirley started giggling again and this time couldn't make herself stop. She had a serious case, laughing louder and louder until all the girls were shushing her.

Finally, Daphne leaned over and shook a finger in her face. "Quiet! The Headmistress may hear you."

Anne and Mary simply fell silent at the mention of the name, but Shirley's eyes went wide. She visibly trembled in the lantern light. "Did you have to say the name? Why did you have to say the name?"

Realizing her mistake, Daphne knelt by her and tried to be calming. "I'm sorry. I'm sorry. You were getting so loud."

"Is she here? Is she coming?"

"No, no, Shirley. Just relax," Mary offered.

"I can't! I can't relax if she might hear me! You told me it was safe!"

Anne leaned forward. "Shirley, look, it *is* safe, if

you relax! So will you shut the hell up?"

Mary's eyes flared. "Anne, that is *not* helping!"

Far off, there was a different sort of noise. It wasn't the usual settling of the old building, or the mysterious scraping of rodents. This sounded more like a far-off door opening. They all heard it, but only Shirley was certain she knew what it was.

"She's coming! She's coming!" Shirley said, panting now like a sick dog. She rose and looked all around. In an animal panic, Shirley ran straight toward a wall with nary a fingerhold to be seen and started to climb it. She skittered up the smooth white wall, higher and higher, not even disturbing the cobwebs, like a moth trying to get through a window.

Then she vanished into the ceiling.

The remaining three girls stared up at the spot where she'd vanished and started calling to it.

"She's not coming!" Daphne said, exasperated.

"There might still be time for another story!" Mary said.

The distant creaking came again, followed by a series of leaden thuds, as if something heavy enough to crush the floor above them was walking on it toward the stairs.

Now they all knew what it was, though none of them bothered to say it. As a cool wind swept the great room, the girls scrambled and shouted.

"Grab the bones!"

"I'll take them!"

"Not you again, Daphne! It's my turn!" said Anne.

The creaking grew louder. It was still wooden at first, but then it seemed like the bricks and mortar were joining in. The whole building creaked and scraped as if aching to speak its pain and rage in words, moaning so loud, it drowned out even the storm.

On the stairs came the tread of heavy feet. The sound grew louder, carrying the dread of punishment nearer. But the true terror only took hold when the sound stopped.

A thin tearful voice whispered, "She's here."

Before the girls could flee, a gust of something cold and terrible hit the oil lamp. In a flash, the small yellow circle of light evaporated as if it had never been there, and a darkness swallowed them all, a great and wonderful darkness that blanketed everything, living and dead, like a coat of rich warm earth packed tightly on a coffin lid.

TO BE CONTINUED

DON'T MISS

WICKED DEAD

TORN

It skittered across the width of the roof, seemed to stumble into a metal vent, then moved steadily, rapidly toward the back.

"Let's go wait in the parking lot," Devin said. "Now."

He started pulling Cheryl toward the side door. One Word Ben was way ahead of them.

Cheryl resisted. "What about Cody?" she said, worried.

He wanted to say, *What about him?*, but instead he

called out across the quiet space. "Cody! Let's get going!"

A muffled slamming sound cried out through the darkness. It could have been the door of a bathroom stall closing. Then there was nothing.

Oh, damn.

"Later," One Word Ben said as he vanished through the door.

Devin's heart thudded its way into his throat. Could it still be the Slits? Cornering them for a final vengeance?

"Cody?" he called, louder.

The slamming came again, followed by a series of thuds. Devin walked toward the middle of the display room, Cheryl beside him.

"Go wait outside," he told her.

"No," she said, annoyed.

Past long rows of brightly colored bureaus and changing tables, he saw the gray men's room door. It was slamming against its frame, rattling as if a fight were going on behind it.

"Cody!" he cried.

A sound came out, low and rough. It could've been Cody calling for help, or it could've been something else entirely. Devin quickened his pace, Cheryl behind him.

Don't miss the next novel in this chilling series!

Daphne, Anne, Shirley, and Mary are rolling the bones once again, while hiding from the evil Headmistress. Tonight's scary tale focuses on seventeen-year-old Devin, whose garage band "Torn" is about to hit the big time. But Devin's pleasant world is ripped apart when a deadly creature appears as though summoned by the band's new song. It violently kills first one, then another of Devin's bandmates . . . Who's next?

HARPER TEEN
An Imprint of HarperCollins Publishers

www.harperteen.com